"What's wrong between us?" Luke asked.

"Something's off, and it has nothing to do with our parents."

The look in his eyes—heat, frustration, determination—sent her heart racing, her breath hitching. He was going to dig until he found out exactly what had gotten into her.

A stupid, dangerous, poorly timed attraction.

She needed to say something instead of standing there struck speechless by his nearness and the rawness in his eyes.

The powerful urge to simply pour it all out, to tell her good friend how she used to feel about him, how she feared she would feel again if she wasn't careful, pulsed in her head. She reached up and laid her hand lightly on his chest. "Luke…"

His eyes sparked, and then he stepped away, his expression turning icy.

The rebuff sent a shock wave of cold through her body, cold enough to knock her back to her senses.

Books by Missy Tippens

Love Inspired

Her Unlikely Family
His Forever Love
A Forever Christmas
A Family for Faith
A House Full of Hope
Georgia Sweethearts
The Guy Next Door

MISSY TIPPENS

Born and raised in Kentucky, Missy met her very own hero when she headed to grad school in Atlanta, Georgia. She promptly fell in love and hasn't left Georgia since. She and her pastor husband have been married twenty-five-plus years now and have been blessed with three wonderful children and an assortment of pets.

Missy is thankful to God that she's been called to write stories of love and faith. After ten years of pursuing her dream of being published, she made her first sale of a full-length novel to the Love Inspired line. She still pinches herself to see if it really happened!

Missy would love to hear from readers through her website, www.missytippens.com, or by email at missytippens@aol.com. For those with no internet access, you may reach her c/o Love Inspired Books, 233 Broadway, Suite 1001, New York, NY 10279.

The Guy Next Door

Missy Tippens

ISBN-13: 978-0-373-81796-2

THE GUY NEXT DOOR

This edition published by arrangement with Love Inspired Books.

www.Harlequin.com

Printed in U.S.A.

Let the peace of Christ rule in your hearts, since as members of one body you were called to peace. And be thankful.

—*Colossians* 3:15

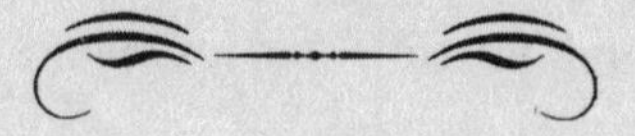

To editors Emily Rodmell and Melissa Endlich—
For allowing me to live my dream.

To Melinda Meredith and Kim Botner—
For lifelong friendship, even across the miles.

To God—
For knowing me fully and loving me anyway.

Acknowledgments:

Special thanks to Rachel Dylan,
Jennifer Artrip Franklin and Olen Winningham
for research assistance.

Thank you to my parents
for their love and encouragement.

Thanks to Lindi Peterson and Janet Dean
for their faithfulness and feedback.
I could never repay you for your help.

To my blogging sisters in Seekerville, thank you for the prayer, daily doses of laughter and loving friendship.

Chapter One

It's about time.

Darcy O'Malley sat on the front porch steps as the hot afternoon sun headed westward, watching her best friend's car pull into the driveway next door. She sucked in a deep breath, tension easing out with it.

Six months. Six *long* months since Luke Jordan had been home—the longest they'd ever gone without seeing each other. Having his car parked where it belonged brought a sense of normalcy.

Of course, these days, he called Tennessee home.

Darcy waved, but he couldn't see her from behind the overgrown boxwoods.

He climbed out of the car and stretched. As expected, his hair had grown shaggy. Unruly brown hair that begged a girl to push it off his forehead.

Darcy gave a derisive snort. It was ridiculous

how many girls had held that honor. Too many to count.

She stepped out on the sidewalk. Luke spotted her and waved, his face lighting with a big goofy grin.

"Come on over," he called, motioning her toward his car.

He met her halfway and held out his arms. She fell into his embrace, wrapping her arms around his neck. When he lifted her off the ground and gave a brotherly squeeze, she felt as if she were the one who had come home. She'd missed him.

"I'm so glad to see you," she said against his cheek, breathing in the familiar scent of his Prell shampoo. "But you need a haircut."

"Glad to be back in Georgia where you can hound me into going to the barber." He set her on her feet and smiled, but his eyes looked shadowed.

She should have anticipated the sadness. This was his first visit home since his mother's funeral. "Tough coming back?"

"Yeah. Seeing the house…" He sucked in a deep breath and glanced up at the two-story brick home he'd lived in from birth.

She waited, knowing better than to push him to talk about his mom.

"I'm surprised to see you here in the middle of the afternoon," he said, effectively changing the subject. "Thought you'd be at one of your many jobs."

Typical of him to slip in a jab about her overpacked schedule, though Luke was simply spouting what everyone else around her had been spouting. He always joked about her overcommitment, but underneath, he was being protective, worried about her stress level and health.

"I only have two jobs," she said. "Finished one for the day and am about to head to the other."

"*Only* two." He shook his head. "You're finally living your dream of being a microbiologist and have the luxury of living rent-free. Why put in so many long hours?"

The muscles in Darcy's neck tightened with nagging concerns over losing that rent-free status before she was ready. "I don't remember asking your opinion," she said, snippier than she'd meant.

One corner of his mouth tilted up in a grin. He'd always loved riling her up and blaming her temper on her red hair.

"Hey, I just want you to have a life," he said. "Maybe go out, have fun, find that Prince Charming you've always dreamed of."

For now, her life was consumed by work and paying off student loans. Even if by some chance Prince Charming did show up, she couldn't squeeze in a moment for him.

She'd missed their banter, though, and couldn't

help returning his smile. "Once again, I don't remember asking for your opinion."

He laughed and nudged her shoulder with his.

"So, how long are you staying?" she asked.

"A week, two at most. I brought some work, and Roger's covering for me."

"Not long, but I'll take what I can get." She hooked her arm around his and looked up. "So when can we hang out?"

Their gazes locked, and his teasing smirk faltered. "Um, I may be pretty busy." He glanced at their joined arms, then at his parents' house.

The action felt like a snub. Had she somehow made him uncomfortable?

"You're not going to like why I'm here," he said.

"Oh?"

"Dad's been talking of downsizing. I'm here to help get the house ready to put on the market. I'm hoping he and Granny will join me in Nashville."

Her heart stuttered. Surely Luke didn't mean it.

He didn't laugh. Didn't bump her shoulder like he usually did when he was joking. Her stomach sank to the sidewalk, and the excitement that had fueled her for days tumbled along with it.

Her best friend might stay in Tennessee permanently?

Stunned, Luke looked into Darcy's eyes—had they always been so blue? Had her auburn hair always been so shiny and silky, her fair, freckled skin so smooth? When she'd wrapped her arm around his, every inch of that smooth skin touching his ignited his nerve endings.

What was wrong with him? This was Darcy. *Darcy.* And she was simply acting like she always did.

He needed to get control of this sudden, weird… attraction. Hadn't he learned the hard way that going from friend to anything beyond friend would end in a mess?

Remember Chloe, he thought, repeating his and Darcy's long-ago mantra. Darcy's sister, Chloe, barely spoke to him nowadays. He couldn't imagine the pain of losing Darcy's friendship.

"It's been six months since you were home, Luke." Darcy glared at him, playful, yet chastising. "Your family can't move away. We'd never see each other."

The hurt tone of her voice made him want to pull her close, to comfort. Instead, he eased his arm out of her grasp. At the moment, even incidental contact left him reeling. "Dad's been depressed, so I need to do something. He's obviously lonely, says the place is too big for him since Mom died."

"It wouldn't be if you moved back to Appleton." The pleading in her eyes was all too familiar. They'd had this conversation several times.

Hands jammed in his pockets, he put extra

space between them. "You've missed me that much, huh?" he teased.

"Dream on." She laughed and hitched a thumb toward the house. "I can't believe your dad would abandon so many memories."

"Once we have a plan in motion to sell the house, I'll ask him to come to Nashville and become a partner in what will soon be my law practice."

She stilled. "You're really going to do it? Stay in Nashville and ask Burt to join you? He's been building his practice here in Appleton for decades. Why don't *you* join *him,* prove yourself like you wanted to do when you were a kid."

That dream had died when his dad had told him he wasn't cut out for law school. When he'd said Luke should probably consider another career. Granted, Luke had goofed off in high school, but midway through college, with Darcy's help, he had buckled down. He'd applied and been admitted into law school the following year. He'd headed to graduate school without his dad's support, and had worked hard to prove Burt wrong.

Looking into her eyes, Luke said, "You know how strongly I feel about making my own way." He nodded toward his car and headed that direction.

"Yeah, I know." She sighed and followed. "I just wish Burt would recognize how good you are at your job. And that *you* would let go of the past and come back here where you belong."

Luke had been working as an associate for Roger Young for nearly a year, had thrived on the challenge and done well. Once Roger retired, Luke would take over. "Business is great. There's more opportunity in the city."

She arched a brow. "Your dad has been very successful in Appleton. Together, you could be more so."

Of course she and the townspeople would assume Luke had gone off on his own and refused an offer to join his father's practice. They didn't know the painful truth. Dad himself didn't even realize how the snub had hurt. "He's never asked me to come work with him."

Darcy's face scrunched in disbelief. "What?"

Luke wished he could take the humiliating words back, but this was Darcy. He could tell her anything. "It's true. Dad never once mentioned having me join his practice, even when I told him about other job offers."

Which had been the death of Luke's dream—Jordan & Jordan, Attorneys at Law in the big Victorian house on Golden Street.

Darcy laid a soft hand on his arm. "I can't believe that."

"You know he doubted me every step of the way, which is why I plan to stay in Nashville."

Luke reached in the backseat and pulled out his luggage.

"Then why ask him to join your practice?"

"I've been worried about him, have been thinking for weeks about asking him to move closer. Figured a new start might help."

She sighed. "I understand your concern. I've been there with Mom."

"I also want to bring in a partner with experience, someone who'll inspire confidence in the clients Roger is sending my way. I'd like to think Dad and I could work well together, especially if I get a chance to show him I'm capable."

As Darcy glanced at her watch, the sun shone on her hair, highlighting coppery strands that brushed well past her shoulders. Most of her life, she'd worn a ponytail. When had she started wearing her hair down? Had it been down the last time he saw her?

"Time to head to the mall job." Eyes so deep blue they sometimes looked violet sparked with frustration. "It doesn't sound as if I'll be able to change your mind about coming back home for good."

Luke shook his head. "I closed on the office building last week. Roger has sent out letters to all his clients informing them of his pending retirement, inviting those who haven't yet worked with me to drop by."

Darcy frowned. "What about your grandmother? You really think she'll move, too?"

That part of his plan didn't sit well with Luke. He hated to uproot Granny after she'd lived in Appleton her whole life. "I hope she will."

"If you ask me, dynamite couldn't blast her out of her home." Her eyes heated before she glanced away, angry. "But, you didn't ask me."

"Come on, Darcy, be happy for me."

"If anyone can persuade Burt and Grace to move, it's their beloved only child and grandchild." Her gaze darted everywhere except directly at him, silently voicing her disapproval, pricking at his conscience.

He hadn't come home looking for approval, though. He'd come home with a goal to help his dad while securing his own future. And he intended to see his plan through.

Luke pushed aside his sadness with each step he took up the ladder leaning against his childhood home. He wouldn't dwell on saying goodbye to the place where he'd grown up. The house was just brick and mortar, full of material stuff. He would always have the memories of his mom.

Darcy would probably disagree. For some odd reason, their earlier conversation had left him rattled. Probably because he'd disappointed her. He'd always hated letting her down.

"What are you doing up there, son?" Burt Jordan, home from the office, stood in the front yard in dress pants and a button-down shirt, sleeves rolled up, arms crossed.

"Trying to get a good look at the roof," Luke said. "Probably needs to be replaced."

"Wish you would've talked to me before you bothered. I've got someone lined up to replace it next week."

Laughing, Luke climbed down. "Good. You're jumping on repairs."

"Noreen has encouraged me to get out of my cave and start living again." Burt held out his hand. "Welcome home."

Luke turned the shake into a brief half hug. "Thanks." He pulled away and took a good look at his dad.

For months after Luke's mom died, Burt had sounded despondent on the phone. The past few weeks, though, he'd sounded stronger, more upbeat. Now, Luke saw a hint of the old spark in his dad's eyes, the way he'd been before Joan got sick. Apparently Darcy's widowed mom, Noreen, had helped Burt begin to deal with the loss.

With a familiar stab of guilt over not being around much the past couple of years, he gave his dad one last pat on the shoulder. "I'm here to help with the house. Tell me what you need."

His dad winced, looking off in the distance,

wrinkles crinkling around his brown eyes. He'd aged a lot since Mom's passing. "Been meaning to talk to you about that."

"I saw the load of pine straw beside the house," Luke said. "Want to spread some mulch while we talk?"

"Sure. Let me change first."

Luke took the ladder to the garage and then located the wheelbarrow. In a few minutes, his dad reappeared in a pair of old jeans and a polo shirt—about as casual as he ever dressed. No faded T-shirts for Burt Jordan. In fact, he rarely wore jeans.

Burt grabbed a shovel and two rakes and handed one to Luke. "Had that load delivered a few weeks ago. Haven't had a chance to spread it."

Either that or he'd been so depressed he hadn't felt up to going outside to work in the yard. "Let's do it, then."

They filled the wheelbarrow and made several trips dumping piles of pine straw around the shrubbery and flower beds, spreading it as they went.

"So are you still wanting to sell the house?" Luke asked.

"Well, the thing is..." Burt raked pine straw around an island of azalea bushes with white blooms almost past their peak. "I've been having second thoughts."

Letting go of the house would be difficult, but if his dad changed his mind about selling, he probably wouldn't consider relocating to Nashville.

Luke stopped raking and rested his arm on the handle. "Is it because of memories of Mom?"

Burt paused and stared off toward the house considering the question, as if unsure how to answer. "That's part of it."

He'd never seen his dad indecisive, but that probably went along with the grief. "Has something changed since you told me you wanted to downsize?"

A look of consternation drew Burt's brows downward. "Selling the house feels so final. It closes the door to the past, and I'm not ready for that. I'd like to do something, first, that'll be a testament to your mom, to show what Joan meant to us and to the community."

Without warning, Luke's throat tightened. "Any ideas?"

"Not yet, although, as active as she was, it shouldn't be difficult. I'm sorry if I dragged you here too soon."

"Don't apologize," Luke said. "I want you to make the right decision for you." And he meant it. No matter what happened with the potential move or partnership, Luke wanted his dad to be happy.

"Life is fleeting," Burt said. "I know I need to move on. I just don't want to rush the process."

Luke pushed the wheelbarrow to spread mulch around the boxwoods in front of the house. "Six months isn't long, and selling is a big decision. I get it."

Burt clapped him on the back. "Exactly. Noreen said you'd understand."

Why would his dad share his doubts with Darcy's mother before he told Luke? The families had been close for ages…but still.

Raking pine straw around the hedges, Luke covered dirt, the occasional weed and remnants of last year's mulch. Noreen was just being supportive. She'd been a widow for a few years. Luke should thank her for being there for Burt. That was what neighbors in Appleton did. They looked out for each other.

Neighbors...Darcy. They'd always looked out for each other, too.

Stopping to wipe his brow, Burt looked around the yard. "I should start dinner soon."

"Go ahead. I'll finish this up."

Burt thanked him and headed inside. In the fading light, Luke hefted one last load of pine straw into the wheelbarrow and pushed it to the opposite side of the house to spread around his mother's rosebushes. He'd have just enough daylight to finish the job.

As he spread mulch around the fragrant plants his mother had tended as if they were her children,

Luke imagined her there beside him. The sweet smell always reminded him of her. The previous week, he'd walked into the office and thought, for a split second, his mom was there. But a vase of freshly cut flowers from Roger's wife's garden had been the trigger.

Joan had been strong and solid, a homemaker who made her family feel loved and cared for, even as she reached out to love others. She'd been the glue that held their family together when he and his dad butted heads through his high school and early college years.

Before Joan died, she told Luke and Burt they needed to be patient with each other, needed to be more supportive. Fortunately, for the most part, he and Burt had made peace. His mother would want that, would expect it.

Luke wanted to join his dad in honoring her memory. Together they would figure out a way.

Tires on the pavement of the driveway next door drew his attention. Darcy returning from her second job?

No. Noreen's small sedan. She climbed out of the vehicle, smiling as she headed his way.

With her long, light blond hair, no gray in sight, and the stylish way she dressed, Noreen had always looked younger than other mothers. Though now, a few slight wrinkles around her light blue eyes hinted at her age.

"Good to have you home," she said as she hugged him. "Burt has looked forward to your visit."

The perfume she wore smelled familiar, as if it was the same perfume his mom, her best friend, had always worn. His throat constricted, forcing him to cough to clear it. "Thanks for all you've done to help him the past few months."

"I know what a struggle it is to lose a spouse. I simply pushed him to get out of the house and back to the office."

"Whatever you've done has worked. He's in a better place."

She started to say something, but then folded her hands together, pressing them in front of her lips as if stopping herself.

"What is it?"

Shaking her head, she smiled. "Nothing at all. Have you seen Darcy yet?"

"Ran into her as I was arriving this afternoon."

Noreen's eyebrows drew together, and she let out a small *humph.* "It's a wonder she was home at all. She's working herself to death to pay off her student loans by a self-imposed deadline. She has no social life."

"I happened to catch her between the lab job and mall job."

Noreen let out a deep sigh. "I told her she is

welcome to continue living with me as long as she likes. No need to push herself so."

He couldn't help but grin. "She always was a little headstrong."

"Just like her dad," she said with a roll of her eyes.

Another vehicle pulled into the driveway. Darcy's SUV. His stomach lurched in anticipation as if he were sixteen instead of twenty-six.

"There she is now," Noreen said. "She works till eight again tomorrow night. Then Saturday, after working all day at the hospital, she'll do the late shift at the mall."

"Late shift?"

"The store closes at ten on weekends, which puts her home after eleven, making for a sixteen-hour day. Added to that, she takes the cash to the night deposit by herself."

By herself with all that money? "Can't she get a security escort?"

"She claims she's perfectly safe."

Darcy joined them by the roses. "From the frown on Mom's face, I'd say she's complaining about my arriving home late."

How could Darcy be so careless? From the time she first moved into a dorm, hadn't he always warned her to be cautious? "She's just worried about you."

Darcy slumped as if exhausted. "I don't need a lecture right now."

"Luke, maybe *you* can talk some sense into her." Noreen rubbed her temples and then headed to the O'Malley house.

Luke turned to Darcy. "Long day, huh?"

"I'm fine. It was a slow evening."

Gently lifting her chin, he examined her face. The shadows pooling under eyes had nothing to do with the fading daylight or harsh outdoor spotlight his dad had turned on. "You look worn out."

"Gee, thanks." She pushed his hand away. "You certainly know how to make a girl feel good."

If he told her how beautiful he thought she was at the moment, she would think he'd gone off his rocker. She would not be comfortable if she found out that just this afternoon he'd seen her through new eyes.

The eyes of a man suddenly aware his best friend was a gorgeous, appealing woman.

Disdain for the out-of-character thoughts sent him grasping for a comeback, something funny, a brotherly dig. As a breeze lifted her long hair, blowing the ends across his arm, all clever thoughts fled.

"Hey, best friends look out for each other, don't they?" he choked out, pulling the best friend card. "Maybe you need an intervention."

"What I need is to have my priorities, my work, respected. You should empathize."

Yeah, he did. But it didn't mean he'd quit worrying about her welfare.

He would head over to the mall late Saturday. Maybe ask her for input on how they could honor his mother. Then he would insist on escorting her to the bank.

It was the least he could do for a friend.

Chapter Two

The next afternoon after a day of work at the lab, Darcy sat across from Grace Hunt, her co-chair for the church's upcoming missions committee auction. She and Grace, who happened to be Luke's grandmother, were working to raise money for the Food4Kids project.

The slamming of a car door outside jerked Darcy's mind away from their discussion.

Grace smoothed her fingers over short, perfectly styled salt-and-pepper hair. "I wonder if that's my grandson arriving at long last?" she said as if ready to shame Luke for waiting twenty-four hours to show up. "Had to invite him to dinner to make sure he'd come see me."

Of course they both knew Luke loved spending time with Grace, and that he could do no wrong in his grandmother's eyes.

Darcy laughed from across the well-worn,

scarred oak table. "I imagine it's him. I think we've covered everything we need to do today."

"We have a good lineup of donors for this year's auction." With her tasteful makeup and up-to-date clothes, Grace looked fifty instead of nearly seventy. The energy and excitement she exuded belied her age, as well.

Darcy pushed away the last bite of the sweet, gooey pecan pie Grace had served. The sounds of birds chirping and a dog barking drifted through the back screen door, tempting Darcy to relax awhile.

She couldn't. The mall job waited. "I should go."

"Oh, I forgot to tell you," Grace said. "Food-4Kids got an anonymous donation today that will cover the budget for the month of May, enabling us to finish out the school year."

"Oh?" Darcy fiddled with the pie plate, staring at it as if it were the most interesting thing ever. "That's great news."

Grace tilted her head toward Darcy, her speculative gaze making Darcy shift in her chair.

"Funny how the donor knew exactly how much we need right when we needed it," Grace said. "Didn't you tell me your new coworker at the hospital—Lois?—has a son who is part of the program and a recipient of the meals? I imagine you'd want to make sure he doesn't go hungry."

Steeling herself, Darcy braved looking at the

oh-so-perceptive woman. "If this year's auction is successful, maybe we won't run out of money next year."

"You sure are generous, especially considering you're working so hard to pay off your college loans."

Darcy's faced burned. She let out a long sigh. "Lois just graduated and is trying to get back on her feet after a divorce. She's adamant about refusing charity, especially from townspeople she knows. So please keep this anonymous, okay?"

Grace made a zipping motion over her lips, but then her grin unzipped them. She patted Darcy's hand. "By the way, I have a plan." She glanced toward the living room to make sure Luke wasn't there.

Apparently that hadn't been his car door they'd heard outside.

Darcy closed the notebook where she'd jotted a list of their project ideas. "Tell me."

Grace clasped her hands in front of her chest, looking more like an excited teenager than a grandmother. "It'll be the perfect way to get through to Luke," she whispered. "My grandson needs a push to get him to move home to Appleton."

No amount of pushing would change Luke's mind now that he'd bought the office building. Apparently, Grace had no idea what Luke planned.

"And that push involves the auction?"

A flash of sadness in Grace's eyes knocked her excitement down a notch. "Since Joan founded the Food4Kids ministry, his helping with the auction would be a connection to his mother."

"Of course."

"I'm simply going to suggest Luke work for a good cause, a cause that meant a lot to Joan."

Darcy herself had experienced moments of sadness at the loss of their committee leader. "You know, I hadn't anticipated how difficult this year's auction would be without her. Are you doing okay?"

Her friend sat straighter, pulling together the edges of her ivory cotton cardigan, taking a deep breath. "I'm fine. And hopeful. I truly think if Luke gets involved in the community, he'll realize this is where he belongs."

Which is exactly what Darcy had hoped, too—before Luke decided to stay in Nashville after law school. "Sure can't hurt to try." She scooted her folder labeled Missions Auction across the table. "He's welcome to take my place on the committee since I don't have a spare minute in my day."

Grace slid the folder back to Darcy. "No, dear. You're part of the plan, too. A reminder that he has friends here."

"Seriously, I don't mind turning over my duties

to him. I've been working fifty to sixty hours a week."

"Working too many hours if you ask me," a deep voice said.

Luke filled the doorway leading to the kitchen, and at the sight of him, her heart gave a stutter.

Heart stutters were not allowed. She raised her chin and gave him a defiant look. "Butting into my business again?"

Grace hopped up and greeted him with a tight hug. "That *was* you we heard out front!"

"I got caught up talking to your neighbors."

"I've missed you, son. 'Bout time you came home."

"Thanks, Granny. I've missed you, too." Over the top of Grace's head he gave Darcy a pointed look. "See, Darcy. That's how you greet a man."

Darcy couldn't help laughing. "Hey, I greeted you like that yesterday, before you started handing out unsolicited advice about my work schedule."

"Come join us." Grace led Luke to the chair beside her. "I was talking to Darcy about her second job."

Grace sat and grasped Darcy's hand, her grip firm and strong. "Your mother told me you're worried about finances. Darcy, honey, you need to find a good man to take care of you. You shouldn't have to shoulder that burden alone."

Darcy almost laughed out loud. Then she remembered Grace had grown up in a different time, had married her husband at eighteen. "I appreciate the thought, but I haven't met my knight in shining armor and can't wait around until I do. I have bills to pay."

"Goodness, dear. How do you think you'll meet the man God intends for you if you're working all the time?" Grace asked.

A problem Darcy had bemoaned for months as her only life outside of work had been fulfilling church obligations.

Darcy glanced at Luke, his rakish grin proof he was enjoying her discomfort over the direction the conversation had taken.

She'd recently accepted the possibility that God planned for her to remain single. Darcy didn't need Grace shaking up a world she'd begun to settle into.

"It's not my place to doubt God's plan for my life." Darcy slid the folder back to Grace. "Now, here. Give this to Luke and tell him about your idea."

"Don't change the subject." Grace eased the folder to Darcy. "It's not your place to assume you know God's plan and give up so easily on love."

"I'm not giving up. I'm simply being realistic."

Back and forth, they'd slid the folder. With each declaration, Luke's questioning gaze bounced between the two of them.

Grace slowly inched the file toward Darcy. "You're a young, beautiful woman with lots to offer, isn't she, Luke?"

As she waited for his response, Darcy's breath froze in her lungs, and she wanted to slap herself silly over the fact that his answer mattered so much to her.

With a smirk on his face, he rubbed his chin and examined her. "She is young, yes..."

Darcy shook her head.

"And has a lot to offer..."

Why did her heart have to beat so wildly? Did she really care what he thought of her?

He leaned forward, his light brown eyes sparkling.

"And...?" She lifted her chin, staring right back, daring him to speak.

The teasing suddenly morphed into something else entirely. The laughter in his eyes heated, holding her captive. The moment seemed to last an eternity.

With one blink, he wiped away the spark between them. He sat back in his chair and looked over at his grandmother. "Granny, I have to admit, now that she's all grown up, she's not hard on the eyes."

The words were something he would typically say in fun, something a brother would jokingly say to disparage his sister. But he appeared to use the words as a weapon against the connection they'd just shared.

A connection they didn't normally have, one that didn't fit best friends.

Fear thudded in her chest. At one time, she'd been one of the many girls with a crush on him. For years, she remained on the sidelines with friend status, watching as Luke dumped girlfriend after girlfriend, marveling at how he somehow managed to remain unscathed and commitment-free, while each new conquest cut her a little deeper. Dating her older sister, Chloe, had been the death of the crush. Falling in love with a girl named Raquel had hammered the nail in the coffin.

She could *not* let herself go there again even for a moment. Luke would end up stomping on her heart like he had before. Unintentionally, granted. But a stomp was painful nonetheless.

Darcy yanked up the auction folder with a huff and pressed it to her chest.

Grace belted out a delighted laugh. "You watch, Darcy. Some lucky young man will come along and snatch you up someday." She winked, crinkles of laugh lines forming around her eyes and mouth, as if daring Darcy to try to get in the last word.

"I surrender," Darcy said. "I'm afraid if I keep refusing this folder, you'll make me arm wrestle Luke to see who has to work on the committee.

Luke, I sure hope you don't plan to refuse your grandmother's plea."

"What plea?" he asked.

"I'll leave you two to talk about it." Darcy tucked the auction notes into her tote bag. "I'm scheduled to work a couple of hours at the mall tonight."

Grace made a tsking sound. "Friday night's the time for a nice dinner date. Didn't I hear that boy Joey up the street asked you out?"

"Joey Meadows?" With twinkling eyes, Luke looked at Darcy, a laugh so close to the surface she wanted to smack him.

"No, Grace. *Joey* didn't ask me out. His mother asked for him."

Luke's bark of laughter bounced off the kitchen cabinets.

"Now, no more pushing me to date. Be thankful I'm leaving with the silly file folder."

"I am thankful. I think you and Luke will do an excellent job co-chairing the auction for the kids in our community."

"What?" he asked.

Darcy's stomach briefly took a nosedive before launching into a fluttery dance. This was Grace's plan? "What do you mean co-chairing?"

"Luke, honey, I need you to take over my duties for the fund-raiser. I'm simply too busy right now to do a thorough job."

"Whoa. Wait a minute," Darcy said. "I thought you were just going to ask him to help." She'd imagined him picking up donated furniture, setting up tables, manual jobs that required a little extra muscle power.

Grace picked up her Bible and waved it. "I'm leading a new women's Bible study group as well as volunteering at the food pantry this month. I'd like to completely hand over the reins to Luke."

"Granny, I—"

She threw her hand up to stop him. "How about we talk more about it over dinner? We don't want to make Darcy late."

"Okay. I'll walk her out."

Maybe Darcy should tell Grace Luke's plan to ask Burt to move. What if they put the house on the market and Luke left next week?

No, Darcy couldn't bear to break the woman's heart. How could she tell Grace that her plan to lure Luke into moving to Appleton was doomed from the start?

Darcy stood and pushed the strap of her bag over her shoulder. "I'll see you on Sunday."

"Thanks for coming, dear. The kids in the community will be blessed by your hard work."

Darcy smiled as she waved and headed toward the living room. Luke went ahead of her and stepped outside to hold the screen door open.

For some reason, the thought of working closely with him on the project made her stomach wrap around itself in a pretzel of dread. So many things could go wrong—namely, the fact that he could leave town at any moment, sticking her with the majority of the auction work.

No, worse was the fact that he didn't seem to care they'd never see each other once he moved Burt and Grace to Nashville.

Barreling out the front door, she ran into a wall of solid muscle.

She nearly bounced off Luke, and he grabbed her arms to set her upright. "You okay?"

"I'm sorry. I was zoned out, wasn't watching."

"In that much of a hurry?"

She looked into his stunning brown eyes and swallowed. Nodded. "Can't be late."

"Working weekend evenings must cut into your social life."

"Not everyone has a hot date every weekend," she snapped.

His eyes widened, and he held up his hands. "Sorry. I meant no offense."

Heat swept from her chest upward. "No, I'm sorry. Sensitive subject after that conversation with your grandmother."

Luke leaned against the screen, trapping her between it and the front door, his lips tilted up in a semi-smile. A knowing, snarky and way-too-appealing smile. "So, no hot dates lately, huh?"

"Spoken by the guy who would date anyone in a skirt." She laughed at his ridiculously cocky pose and tried to shove him out of her way.

His bulging biceps didn't budge.

A growl formed in her throat, but she stifled it. "Some of us are more selective than others," she said instead, staring him down, wondering at her breathlessness. What was wrong with her?

"Touché." His gaze dipped to her lips.

Great. A smudge of pecan pie filling or a speck of crust must've landed on her mouth. She nonchalantly wiped the area, just in case.

Luke laughed and stepped back, holding the screen door open. "I'm just playing with you. So you're heading to the mall job?"

The extra space between them gave her room to breathe. "A night of selling accessories to the teen crowd at Glitzy Glenda's. Have to be there at six." Still trying to gather her wits, she glanced at her watch. "It's five-thirty already."

"Oh, well, I won't keep you. But I do need your input on a matter with my dad. Maybe we can get together this weekend?"

Before she could decide how to answer, he gave a jaunty salute and headed back inside, totally unaffected by their close encounter.

* * *

Luke stepped inside Granny's house, closed the front door and let his head drop against it. *Man, what's my problem?*

Darcy was acting perfectly normal, but he hadn't been able to since the previous day when she'd first smiled up at him and it hit him how badly he'd missed her.

The last time he was home, Darcy had been his rock, holding his hand through his mom's funeral and graveside service. Talking to friends and family whenever he choked up, sensing his every need. They'd been more in tune than ever.

As friends. So what had changed?

Maybe he'd been working too hard. Hadn't been on a date in ages. That had to be the problem. Easily remedied when he got back to Nashville.

Luke shook off the weirdness and headed back to help with dinner.

Bustling around her kitchen, his grandmother tried to fill the space—space his mother would normally fill—with chatter.

Everything felt wrong without Mom in their midst. Empty-chair wrong. Lack-of-her-voice wrong. And wrong for Grace to be preparing dinner without the help of her daughter.

Desperate to ease the emptiness, Luke touched

his grandmother's shoulder. "Will you show me how to make your chicken casserole?"

With a grateful smile and misty eyes, she nodded. "Of course."

As Granny continued making his favorite dish, she jotted down the recipe and talked him through the preparation. Pulling boiled chicken off the bones and chopping vegetables somehow soothed both of them. Granny chatted about the townspeople and church friends to update him on all the latest news. When she finally popped the casserole in the oven, she settled him at the table next to a freshly baked pecan pie with two slices missing. His mouth watered.

"There's your dessert," she said as she sat across from him with a satisfied smile.

"You know, you're making life tough for my future wife."

"I love spoiling you, and having you back home where you belong." Her brown eyes shone with happiness. Time together was good for both of them.

Unfortunately, his ultimate goal would not make her happy. "Granny—"

"Before you tell me everything that's going on with you, I need to talk to you about heading the auction committee."

"I won't be in town long."

She pushed herself up from the table and

grabbed the calendar off the wall. The month of May featured a photo of kittens and puppies snuggled up together. Typical Granny.

As she returned to her seat, she spun the calendar around so he could see the blocks of writing. "You may not know it, but I'm a busy woman. Thought my senior years would be slow-paced and relaxed, but I hardly have a spare moment."

Her scribbles on the calendar indicated committee meetings and Bible studies and luncheons. Other than Sunday, she barely had a day open each week. Had she guessed why he was in town and wanted to make it clear that she'd never willingly move away?

"Wow. Looks like you've got your hand in everything around town."

"I do. I like feeling needed. And like that I can contribute, giving back to my community and church."

He nodded and swallowed hard. *Here it comes. She's onto my plan and is going to scold me for it.*

"That's why I need your help," she said. "Your timing is perfect for this project." Her smile gentled. "The purpose of the auction is to raise funds for Food4Kids, the program your mother started."

He pulled in a long, slow breath, trying to control his emotions. "I remember her working on it." He'd hated to imagine kids having the kind of gnawing hunger that made your stomach dig into your backbone.

"When Joan first started Food4Kids at the elementary schools, the number of kids whose parents weren't willing or able to provide nourishing meals on weekends was small. No more than ten children. But a growing number come to school on Mondays hungry."

"How many are in the program now?" he asked.

"Over a hundred kids countywide. More on a waiting list."

"And you need more funding." His mother's face formed in his mind. He recalled her working diligently for those children, making sure each one went home on Friday afternoons with a backpack full of food to keep them until Monday's breakfast at school. She would be pleased to have his help on her pet project.

If Luke took over this auction and saw it through, the funds would help the community, and possibly comfort his grandmother.

Ensuring this program continued would honor his mother. Perhaps help his dad to heal. "Granny, tell me what I can do."

Squeezing his hand, she blinked back tears. "You're a kindhearted man, Luke. I'm proud of you."

She wouldn't be so proud when he offered his

dad a job in Tennessee. Or when he asked Granny if she'd consider joining them.

Grace popped up out of her chair once again and grabbed a spiral-bound notebook from the small desk near the pantry. She set it in front of him. "Here are all the ideas Darcy and I have jotted so far. And a preliminary list of individual and business donors."

"Darcy has all this info, too?"

"Yes, she's been my co-chair and has worked on the committee for a couple of years."

"Good. She can get me up to speed. I plan to see her this weekend."

"Perfect." She shoved the notebook into his hands. "The job's all yours."

Later, though, after Burt joined them for dinner and Luke had time to reflect on the arrangement with Darcy, he had a moment of doubt. Six months ago—six days ago, even—he would have said working with Darcy would be fun. He would have been pleased to spend time with his best friend. Content to relive the times they worked together on school or church projects.

But now, he felt uneasy.

He thought of the spark that zipped between them earlier, across the table and again at the front door. Thought of Darcy's greeting the other day, falling into his arms, so glad to see him. The flowery smell of her silky auburn hair, the brush of her arm against his as she looked up at him, caring, trusting.

Yeah, the trusting part must be what was unsettling him.

He'd come to help his dad prepare to move. Period. He couldn't let his thoughts run to what Darcy expected from him, or of any disappointment she'd shown over his plan.

While sitting at the workbench Saturday afternoon, Darcy's stomach growled. Loudly.

Lois, her coworker in the microbiology lab, giggled. "Almost ready for lunch?"

"All done." Darcy stacked petri dishes in a large bin and slid it back into the incubator. She enjoyed her full-time job at the local hospital. Loved the challenges each day offered, loved knowing her work helped patients even though she didn't have direct contact with them.

"You want to go to lunch first?" Lois asked.

"I've still got to enter culture results into the computer."

Darcy pulled over the portable keyboard to record the Saturday morning data. When she got to the last patient, she entered "Light growth beta hemolytic Strep. Isolated for typing and sensitivity."

This particular patient had been septic. Darcy

prayed the organism they'd discovered on a Gram's stain yesterday wouldn't show antibiotic resistance.

"Darcy, there's someone out front asking to see you." Dr. Violet Crenshaw, the new pediatrician in town who often came by the lab on weekends to check test results of her patients, stood in the doorway of the microbiology lab. "And he's gorgeous," she said in a singsong voice.

"Thanks. I'll be right there." The mystery man had to be Luke. She'd always gotten that kind of reaction when she introduced him to friends at college or work.

Lois popped up from the microscope and hurried around the workbench. "So? Who is he?"

"No reason to get excited. I'm sure it's only Luke, an old friend of mine."

She wiggled her eyebrows. "Only a friend?"

"My best friend since birth."

"Ooh, is he single?" she practically purred.

"No." Shock jolted through Darcy at the sharp tone she'd used. "I mean, yes. I assume he is."

Lois's surprised expression confirmed her abruptness.

"I'm sorry. Anyway, he lives in Nashville now," she added stupidly.

"If he's only a friend, maybe you can introduce us sometime. I love Nashville." Lois wiggled her eyebrows and headed back to the scope.

"Sure."

Why did I do that? Lois and Luke would actually be a good match. She was cute and fun. A little quiet, but not afraid to belt out a good laugh when warranted. And she was a struggling single mom with a young son who could use a good man in his life. Luke would like her sweetness. Her generosity. Her dark brown eyes and wavy blond hair.

Luke had always been partial to blondes with brown eyes.

By the time Darcy reached the lab waiting area, workers whispered and checked him out. She was irked that Luke had garnered the interest of every female in the lab.

She tried to exhale her irritation as she approached, brushing her not-blond hair out of her not-brown eyes.

"Hi, Darcy. I saw you back there in the lab, looking professional in that lab coat," Luke said.

"Yeah, it's a real fashion statement, all right."

"I'm serious. You worked hard to get here."

Her stomach tumbled and twirled, pleased he'd noticed. "Thanks. So, what's up?"

"Looks like we'll be working together on the Food4Kids auction."

"So you're definitely taking Grace's place?"

"I figured it's the least I can do to honor my mom. And I have some ideas. Wanted to see if you'd like to have lunch to discuss them."

Still hesitant to spend too much time with him, yet certain she could handle it, she gave a firm nod. "It's a great way to honor your mom. I was just about to take my lunch break."

He held up a bag from the local sub sandwich shop. "Brought your favorite."

"You don't know my favorite anymore."

He widened his eyes at her, looking quite pleased with himself. "Really? You don't give me enough credit."

"I no longer order ham and cheddar."

"No ham and cheddar with mayo, mustard and tomato?" he asked with a cocky grin.

She shook her head, admittedly pleased he at least remembered her old favorite. "See? You've been gone too long. Things have changed."

"Then I'm glad I ordered you the turkey and Swiss instead. With light mayo, honey mustard, spinach and green peppers."

"How on earth?"

He shrugged and glanced across the room awkwardly. "I care enough to find out what you like."

Her stomach swooped up and around, doing a few curlicues in the region of her heart. She opened her mouth but, unable to find words, she snapped it shut.

The fact that he knew her new favorite sandwich really should *not* make her so happy. She was acting ridiculous.

Luke suddenly gave her a big flirty wink—a Luke Jordan trademark, as if the whole embarrassment thing had been for show. "I also had to promise Mike a place to stay when he comes up for a concert in Nashville."

Of course. Mike. The owner of the sub shop where she'd eaten regularly for the past year.

She snatched the bag out of his hand with a laugh. "You're incorrigible."

"The weather is perfect. Let's go outside."

She joined him as they headed outside to a picnic table near a walking path for employees.

As he set out the sandwiches and chips, she realized she hadn't been on a picnic since their college days. They'd frequently eaten together while studying, sometimes in the quad on a blanket. Of course, their last picnic had been a disaster.

"The last picnic I had was when we ate pizza outside the dorm during finals senior year," he said.

Why did he always seem to know what she was thinking as if their brains were somehow connected? "Me, too. And you ruined that one by bringing along what's her name." Which had hurt Darcy's feelings. Before that day, they'd always kept their friendship separate from dating relationships, had protected their time together.

He grinned and held his hand over his heart.

"You wound me. You don't even remember her name."

Snorting a laugh, she reached for the can of Coke he'd sat in front of her and popped the tab. "You probably don't, either."

He belted a hearty laugh as he pulled Grace's notebook out of the bag and flipped it open. Then he attacked the wrapping on his ham sandwich. "I think an auction is a great idea for a fund-raiser, but I wonder if maybe we should do more this year. Maybe host a dinner or even a formal dance to coincide."

She threw her hand up. "Whoa. I only signed on for the auction, which has always included a covered-dish dinner right after church. What you're suggesting sounds like a ton more work. As it is, I barely have time to breathe."

"I figured we might as well give attendees other opportunities to contribute. No matter what we end up doing, I'd like to have a special time to honor my mother."

She envisioned table decorations, caterers, a band. "All great ideas. Honoring Joan would be fantastic. But I can't let this project eat into my part-time hours at the mall. If you want to do a dinner or dance, maybe I could talk Chloe into taking over for me. She has a lot of business contacts in town."

His nose scrunched. "That might not go well."

No, he and her sister hadn't gotten along since he'd pursued her one summer in college. Luke finally captured Chloe's heart—breaking Darcy's—but the big breakup later that fall ruined his and Chloe's friendship.

"You're both adults now," Darcy said. "Surely you could work together for charity." Yes, they were all adults. So how could the mere suggestion that he work with Chloe still hurt?

"I'd rather work with you." He looked into her eyes, and like some kind of terrible magnet, his gaze tugged at her heart.

Losing herself in those amazing brown eyes was an all-too-familiar feeling. Even at twenty-five, she was still vulnerable to his charm.

She couldn't allow it. He would distract her. Hurt her. She had to stay focused on her goals.

"We'll have to work around my two schedules." Darcy forced her attention to her sandwich. She needed to work the two jobs to pay off student loans early so she didn't have to rely on her mother. Noreen was finally acting happy again, and Darcy suspected she'd been seeing someone. She needed to give her mom some space, and despite what Grace said, Prince Charming wouldn't just show up to sweep her off her feet.

Darcy glanced across the table. Luke with his flirty winks and his flattering words would only set her heart down the wrong path.

"Let's just stick to doing the auction and lunch. We can manage." He slapped his hand on the notebook. "So, have you looked at the list of tentative donors?"

"I helped compile it. Now we need to call each one to confirm and arrange a time to pick up the items. We can split the names."

"I can do the calling. I'll be around the house helping Dad, so my schedule will be flexible."

"Sounds good. I've already arranged to pick up an unassembled portable basketball hoop from Mr. Lipscomb at the sporting goods store. Can you help with that on Sunday after church?"

"Sure. I'll see if I can arrange some other donation pickups for Sunday afternoon since we'll already be out."

Oh, goodness. She thought of all the hours she, Grace and Joan had spent together on this project over the years. "We need to meet soon to approve the quarter-page newspaper ad, and to try to land some radio spots. Also we have to set up the fellowship hall. We'll have quite a few late evenings."

"No problem." He smiled, then, distracted by his food, he took a big bite of his sandwich.

As they finished their lunch, she told him a little something about each of the donors, and about the Colorado ski trip that had been donated, their big-ticket item. By the time he walked her back inside the hospital, they had a basic game plan.

With the notebook in one hand and the other shoved in his pocket, Luke studied her. "I know how hard you work, Darcy. You give a hundred percent to everything you do. I'll try my best to make the auction work easier on you, to keep it from eating away all your free time."

He looked so serious. So earnest. From flirty charmer to sweet, caring best friend in the span of a lunch break. Both equally appealing, neither safe for her heart.

But Food4Kids needed her. Needed them as a team.

For the kids, and against her instinct for self-preservation, she would spend time with her friend. She could do this. "Thanks, Luke. I look forward to working with you."

Chapter Three

Fifteen minutes to closing time. Darcy glanced around Glitzy Glenda's, empty of customers, hoping to make it an early night. Maybe a few minutes to read that novel that sat untouched, gathering dust on her nightstand?

She folded one last scarf and placed it neatly on top of the stack, enjoying the sense of accomplishment that came with tidying up. Saturday nights could sometimes be a nightmare, but an older crowd had hit earlier than usual. Though she enjoyed working with preteens and young teenagers, they tended to travel in packs, tearing through the place like a tornado, leaving a swath of destruction in their wake. Something Darcy couldn't relate to at all.

She'd never had a pack of girlfriends in high school. Never enjoyed shopping for jewelry, purses and hair accessories. She'd been tomboyish, a late bloomer who'd spent all her spare time with Luke, fearing he'd see her differently if she suddenly showed up wearing dangly earrings and eyeliner.

Certain he'd never think her as pretty as Chloe.

Shaking off old memories, she headed toward the cash register. One last quick walk around the shop and—

The entrance chime sounded. A group of giggling girls set upon tables of jewelry, and Darcy's hope for an early evening quickly fizzled. "May I help you girls?"

One, a redhead with pretty hazel eyes set off by the perfect application of makeup, fastened a double strand of faux pink pearls around her neck and admired it in a mirror. "We're just looking."

Two of her friends, squealing at fifty decibels, darted to a table of wristlets.

"Oh, look," screeched one. "The exact shade of green as my new Keds!"

"Buy it. Have you got your mom's debit card on you?"

"Yeah."

"Ashley, wait. Come look at this one first," called a girl from the other side of the store.

Meanwhile, two others stacked bracelets up the arms of a third friend.

There appeared to be a half-dozen of them dressed in stylish clothes, their hair about the same length and all flat ironed. At some point that evening, they'd eaten at a nearby restaurant because several of them had to-go cups they'd set down and quickly forgotten.

She closed her eyes and let out a sigh as the image of that novel beside her bed faded into oblivion.

A crash sounded in the back. "Uh-oh," said one of the girls.

Crashes followed by uh-oh's were never a good thing.

Darcy rushed to the back and found a rack of earrings turned over and gold and silver hoops scattered across the floor.

"I'm so sorry." The girl's mortified expression sent her friends into a fit of laughter.

"Don't worry about it," Darcy said.

While the three girls meandered to the next table, chattering and playing around as if nothing had happened, Darcy scooped up packs of earrings. The chime sounded again as someone else entered. *Great.*

"I'll be right there," she called.

The last of the earrings had landed under the display case. She got on her hands and knees and, with a grunt, made one last-ditch effort to reach them.

"Need some help?"

Luke. And she heard the grin in his voice.

"Luke Jordan, if you were a real gentleman, you'd already be down here helping me."

"You're right. My apologies." He chuckled as he knelt down beside her and reached underneath the display, his breath tickling her neck as he angled his head out of the way.

She bolted to her feet. "A pack of…uh…earrings. Do you feel it?" She touched her neck. How many times had they wrestled around or goofed off without her ever once thinking about the feel of his breath against her skin?

And now—

"Is this what you're looking for?" He stood and handed her the earrings.

"Yes. Thank you." The fact he could set her on edge made her angry. At herself. And, though unfair, at him.

She tugged her shirt back where it belonged. Straightened the collar. "I need to check on my customers."

"Go ahead. I'll wait at the cash register."

She caught up with the six girls near the front and tried to feign calmness she didn't feel at the moment. "Are y'all ready to check out?"

"I think so." The redhead still wore the necklace.

"So you decided to go with the pink pearls? They look great on you."

She fingered them, looking around at her friends for confirmation. "I do like them."

"They're too classy for you," said one of her supposed friends with a sneer before turning to the brunette nearby and laughing.

The girl looked stricken as she removed the necklace. "But they're kind of expensive."

"Come on, let's get out of here and see if the yogurt place is still open," said the mean one. She was the obvious leader, because everyone followed without questioning her order.

They also left without purchasing anything. Instead, they all set their items on a table near the door before quickly exiting to catch up with their boss.

Darcy growled as she rolled down the metal gate that closed off the shop from the mall.

"Tough night?" Luke asked.

"A little slower than usual, but that last group was typical. I'm afraid I'm not good at sales with the younger crowd." She nodded to the discarded items. "They were going to buy those, but the pack leader declared it was time to go."

"Next time, tell her to back off."

Darcy laughed. "I'm sure that would go over really well. I'd probably get reported to my boss by a credit-card-toting teen."

His eyes sparkled with mischief, as if he'd love to see the event. "Yeah, but you might make the sale."

The main problem was that all these girly things were new to her, something she'd always been too embarrassed to admit she loved and longed to wear. "You know me. This feminine stuff is a steep learning curve."

He looked her up and down with an intensity that made her squirm.

"You look plenty feminine to me. A natural beauty. You don't need all this sparkly—" he gestured around the shop "—paraphernalia."

Stunned, Darcy looked into his eyes. He'd always complimented her on being smart, but never had he praised her looks or femininity. Even that afternoon at Grace's, he hadn't said she was pretty.

"Accept the compliment, say, 'Thank you,'" he teased, his smile softening.

Flames crept up her neck. "I need to clean up this mess." The pink pearl necklace clacked as she jerked it up and hung it on the display.

"Fine. Ignore me."

"I'm not ignoring you." Darcy snatched up the neon green wristlet the girl had left behind and headed to the table of spring clearance items. "I don't tend to trust compliments from a man who's said those words to half the female population."

He followed, laying a hand on her arm to still her movements. "I wasn't giving you some cheap, recycled line. I spoke the truth, a truth you need to take to heart."

What Darcy needed to take to heart at the moment was the fact she had to be careful around him, especially when he was being kind and supportive.

Being a good friend.

Darcy was strong and capable. Why go all weak-kneed just because he said she's a natural beauty? "I accept your compliment."

Luke smiled, a victorious smile. "Good. While we're having this heart-to-heart, let me add that I hate seeing you killing yourself working two jobs when you don't need to, and then volunteering at the church on top of it."

Picking up the last of the discarded items, Darcy headed to the other side of the store. "You've already stated your opinion. And as I've already told you, I need to pay off my college debt to prepare to live on my own."

"Your mom is worried about you, and so am I."

"Did my mom send you?"

"It was my idea to come tonight."

But he hadn't denied her mother's involvement. Whether or not she had sent him, Luke hadn't come by because he wanted to spend time with her. "Ah, I see. You dropped by to make sure I don't get robbed making the deposit."

"Your mom mentioned you carry cash to the bank each time you close."

Darcy shook her head. "I appreciate you caring,

but I'm perfectly safe. The night deposit drop box is located inside the front entrance of the mall, so I don't even leave the premises with money."

He ran a hand through his hair, causing a curl to drop across his forehead. "And you refuse to call mall security to escort you?"

"I walk with employees from several other stores." *When the timing works out.*

"All of you sitting ducks, targets for someone armed and possibly desperate."

Frustrated that he didn't seem to be listening to her, she marched to the front of the store and raised the gated door. "You can either trust my judgment, or you can leave."

"I'm not leaving."

"Then don't show up when it suits you and start butting into my business. You're not my keeper."

Color streaked across his cheekbones, a sure sign he was majorly frustrated. His jaw sawed back and forth. "No, I'm not. I'm your friend. Your *best* friend. And that should count for something."

Of course, he had to go and play the best friend card. They rarely did, only in dire circumstances. Darcy had pulled it once when he was dating a girl who ended up in juvie. He'd used it when she'd been sixteen and made plans to attend a party where there would be drinking, and another time when an overly charming lead singer of a band had asked her out in college.

He must be truly worried about her safety.

Begrudgingly, she reclosed the gate. "Wait here."

Once again, his victory smile flashed, but at least he had the decency not to verbally gloat.

"I won't be long closing out the cash register since we hardly sold anything." She sighed. "If I can't make the sale when these hoards of kids show up on the weekends, I'm afraid my boss will fire me."

"And that would be a bad thing because…?"

His sarcastic grin made her smile, too. "Oh, hush."

Leaving him to *guard* the place, she batched out the credit card machine, counted the cash and checks and filled out the deposit slip. She tucked the deposit in a lockable bank bag and then placed the cash register drawer, holding a set amount of money for the morning shift, in the safe.

Darcy quickly collected the to-go cups the girls had abandoned and emptied the trash. "I'm ready."

Luke took the trash bag from her, dumped it in a large rolling bin mall management provided near the shop entrance, and then waited in the mall as she turned off the lights, set the alarm, pulled down the gated door and locked it. He looked around, alert, ready to defend her.

She laughed, but his action set up an ache in her chest that haunted her all the way to the night deposit box. She loved that he cared about her. Yet she longed for more.

Longed for something Luke couldn't provide.

With a flourish, she tossed the money bag in the bank depository and closed the door, proving her shop closing ritual was safe.

He scowled at her flippant action. "I really don't like the idea of you doing this several times a week."

"Then I guess you'll have to move back home and escort me each night." She smiled sweetly, though the idea actually held appeal. Would he reconsider coming home?

His intense stare, as if he was possibly considering that option, made her heart race.

"You could do it, you know," she said.

One side of his mouth hitched up. "Be your bodyguard each night?"

"No. Move back home. Open your own practice here."

He shook his head as he opened the mall door, holding it for her. She pointed to her car, and they headed that direction.

"Can I ask you something without you getting in a huff about it?" he asked.

Which proved how well he knew her. "Probably not."

His familiar chuckle, and the fact they'd been

friends forever, made her miss the past, less complicated times.

"Why are you in such a hurry to move into your own place?" he asked. "Why not take your time, be a companion for your mom and give up the overtime?"

"I told you. I need to prepare to move out, to support myself. And having the student loans over my head stresses me out."

"I can tell you're worried about more than that."

How could she explain her need to be financially independent in case she never married? "Mom needs her house and her life back. Needs her privacy, because I think she may be seeing someone. I should move on soon, but with bills to pay and no one to help me, I have to first plan and save."

"Your mom would help if you needed her to," Luke said.

"Sure, mom would let me live with her if I got in a jam. Even so, I need to be capable of supporting myself and don't have any backup plan like you do."

His eyes narrowed. "Backup plan?"

"If your business fails, your grandmother would help out, like she paid for graduate school."

He straightened, offended. "My business isn't going to fail."

Her heart lurched. He'd always been sensitive

about succeeding despite his dad's doubts. "Of course it's not going to fail. I only meant—"

"There's your car," he said coolly, cutting off her explanation. "I want to make sure you're locked inside before I leave."

Oh, man. She'd really made him mad. "Thanks for seeing me out safely." She climbed in and locked the door.

He turned and walked away.

I'm such a rotten friend.

Luke rarely got mad. And when he did, it blew over quickly. But this time he was more than angry. She'd hurt him right where he was most vulnerable.

On Sunday morning as the congregation rose for the closing hymn for morning worship, Luke glanced at his dad beside him. They were standing in their regular pew in the middle of the sanctuary. Granny stood on the other side of Burt, singing her heart out.

All Luke could think about was that he needed to find a seasoned business partner—preferably his dad—and soon. He'd checked email that morning before leaving for the church and found a message from a client who had decided to leave the firm when he learned of Roger's retirement, wanting a more experienced trial lawyer. And he wasn't the first. Several others had already contacted Roger with concerns the past couple of days.

Luke tried to force his mind back to the music, to words that should inspire him and prevent his mind from wandering.

Staring at the hymnal, Luke recalled Darcy's words from the night before. Did she truly think his business would fail? That he wasn't capable of seeing it through the transition after Roger's retirement?

The thought stung, but with his lack of work experience, she could be right. He couldn't control whether clients left the firm. But he could control whom he hired and how he ran his business.

As Luke stared at the words on the page, the letters running together, he couldn't help wondering what people would think of him asking his dad to come to Tennessee to join his practice. Would they think Luke hadn't been able to succeed on his own?

No, he would be offering Burt an opportunity to start over. Thanks to Roger, Luke would be the one bringing clients to their new partnership.

As they filed out after the service, the elderly, squat gray-haired pastor of Appleton Community Church greeted parishioners at the door. Ever since Luke had moved to Nashville, he'd missed hearing sermons. Mainly because he spent Sundays at the office.

That needed to change. He needed to put God first in his life. He should find a place he felt as comfortable as he did in his Appleton church and attend worship more faithfully.

With light filtering through the stained glass windows, Luke inched along the carpeted center aisle with his dad and grandmother, greeting old friends. He hadn't seen any of them since his mother's funeral, and a few mentioned once again how sweet and fitting the service had been. Their comments made it difficult for Luke to speak.

Each time someone said something about Joan, Luke glanced at his father, wondering how he managed to hold himself together. Burt simply shook their hands and agreed.

Once they greeted the pastor and exited the church, Granny headed to speak with a friend.

"Dad, has this talk about Mom been hard for you?" Luke asked.

"It was tough when I first came back to church. In fact, I doubt I'd be back if it wasn't for Noreen pushing me. Too many memories. That empty seat beside me."

"And now?"

Burt stood straight and determined, chin held high. "I'm always going to miss your mother, but she wanted me to live my life. I'm pushing through, trying to keep going."

Glad his dad was doing better, Luke nodded.

Yet Luke worried his dad could be trying so hard to move on that he was in denial, not truly dealing with the grief.

"There's Noreen now." Burt waved to her and Darcy as they came out the door.

The way Burt's face lit up right before he bounded toward the women set off a warning signal in Luke's brain. Dad and Noreen?

No way.

Noreen had been his mother's best friend for decades. Their families had spent summers together at a lake house they first rented and then purchased together as co-owners. The adults had played Monopoly on Friday nights and went to movies together. The men had gone on fishing trips. The women swapped recipes and shopped.

There was no way his dad and Noreen would get involved romantically. Like Luke and Darcy would never get involved.

That had to be gratitude Luke had witnessed in Burt's eyes. Gratitude for pulling him out of his isolation and depression.

As Granny approached, she watched Burt. Grace was very perceptive. If anything were going on between Burt and Noreen, she would notice.

Snapping her attention to Luke, she smiled. "Ready to go?"

Apparently she hadn't picked up on anything.

Luke took his grandmother's arm and led her to join the others.

Burt waved them closer. "Luke, Darcy told me you're helping pick up a basketball hoop for the auction."

Darcy's face flushed. She looked breathtaking in her deep blue blouse that matched her eyes exactly. She also wore a slim-fitting, knee-length skirt, a far cry from her casual college attire.

He liked this new, feminine look. Liked how the skirt showed off her slim legs, how—

Cut it out, Jordan. He pulled his attention back to his father. "I'm actually going to be working with Darcy on the fund-raising committee for Food4Kids while I'm home."

"You are?" Dad asked, a broad smile forming. "Good to hear. Your mom would be pleased."

"That's nice of you, Luke," Noreen said. "Hey, why don't y'all plan on coming back to the house this evening for dinner? Grace, you, too. And Burt, of course," she added almost as if she'd forgotten him, her cheeks turning bright red.

Once again, alarm bells clanged in Luke's head. Since when did Noreen blush around anyone in his family? Had she developed a crush on his father?

"We'd be delighted to come," Dad said, totally oblivious to the undercurrents.

Poor Dad. Letting Noreen down easy would be difficult. And not something Burt should have to deal with. Maybe Darcy could have a talk with her, gently suggest she be careful with her feelings.

Grace patted Noreen's arm. "Thank you, dear, but I'm helping cook supper for the youth group kids tonight. I'll join you another time."

"Luke, I guess we need to head on over to the sporting goods store," Darcy said.

"Sure."

They said their goodbyes and walked to her small SUV.

"I appreciate this. I know you're probably still angry with me," she said as she pulled out of the parking lot.

"Angry with you?"

"Oh, come on. It's me here. Don't act like you don't know what I'm talking about."

So much for blowing off her comment from the night before. "Yeah, well…"

"I'm sorry. I really do believe in you. You've worked hard, accomplished so much." She glanced over at him, her eyes begging him to believe her. "I *know* you won't fail."

As long as he could remember, she had believed in him and never wavered. That support was one of the reasons her friendship was so important to him. How could he stay mad at her? Besides, he'd never been able to. All she ever had to do was smile or laugh and it set his world right. "Forget about it."

"Thanks." She glanced over and gave him one of those smiles, soothing his bruised ego.

"So what's the deal with your mom liking my dad?" he asked.

The car gave a lurch as she pushed the gas pedal too hard. "What?"

"I think she may have a crush on him. He's been talking about Noreen this and Noreen that, as if she's been helping him through his grief. From the way she was blushing just now, I think maybe she's got feelings for him."

Flipping on the blinker, Darcy glanced at him. "That's crazy. They're friends."

"Have they been spending more time together?"

"I don't really know. I'm not home much."

Which meant it was entirely possible. He chewed the inside of his cheek as he considered what all Burt and Noreen might have talked about, might have shared. "You know, Dad says he's having second thoughts about moving out of the house. Could be that she's discouraging it."

"I don't see why she'd do that unless she thinks it's too soon for him to make that type of decision. I remember her having fleeting thoughts about selling the house right after Dad died. Later, she said she was glad she hadn't."

Which only made asking his dad to relocate more difficult. "Maybe that's all it is, a friend advising a friend. Still, you might want to talk to her. I'm afraid she'll end up getting hurt."

"You don't need to worry. Remember, I think she may be seeing someone." Darcy stopped at a stop sign and looked over, irritation drawing her mouth downward. "What if they did care for each other? Would that be a bad thing?"

How could she even entertain the idea? "Oh, come on, you can't be serious. That would be strange. She was my mom's best friend."

"She's been talking on the phone to someone a good bit, comes in late at night without explanation. Your dad would be a whole lot better than some stranger she's apparently hiding from me."

"Remember Chloe," he said, reminding her of the mantra they'd typically used when one of them kidded about dating the other. "Applies to our parents, as well."

She gave him an apologetic close-lipped smile. "Still, weird or not, I'd pick your dad over her dating someone I haven't yet met."

He shook his head. Time to get back to the business at hand. "I made some calls yesterday to confirm donations. Have a pretty good-size list for us today, so we might want to drive through and grab lunch at some point."

She pulled into the sporting goods store lot and turned off the car. Held out her hand. "Show me the list. I can set up our route for efficiency."

Darcy had always been one to jump in any situation and get right to work. A trait he'd admired. A trait that would serve them well for the fundraiser. He needed to set aside any difference of opinion over their parents.

"We make a good team," he said. "I appreciate you helping me."

When she gave him a self-satisfied smirk, it was as if the old Darcy had fully returned. A teasing glint lit her eyes as she leaned over the console and squeezed his biceps. "I suppose you do need my help with heavy items. Office work makes you soft."

"And microscope work is muscle-building?" Laughing, he returned the inspection, his hand easily wrapping around her slim upper arm. The delicate skin was so soft that he couldn't resist rubbing his thumb over the underside.

She sucked in a breath, and it was as if the intake changed the electron composition of the air in the car. The space sizzled with tension as they stared into each other's eyes. His heart began to thud, quick and strong.

"Um, yeah, lifting all those test tubes and petri dishes is a real workout." With a strained laugh, she pulled away from his grip and clenched her hands in her lap.

Remember Chloe.

"So. A portable basketball hoop, huh?" he choked

out. "That should bring in quite a few bucks for the kids."

"Yes. Valued at one hundred seventy-nine dollars."

"Very nice, indeed." He had to get out of the car before he said something stupid. He threw open his door, allowing all the awkwardness to escape the vehicle. "Come on. We've got a lot to do today."

If Darcy didn't get a grip, this working with Luke was going to be torture. Pure torture.

She strengthened her resolve and somehow managed to get through the day. But it seemed as if every five minutes her mind would wander, and she'd recall his touch.

At dinnertime, she pulled her SUV, full of the items they'd picked up that afternoon, into her driveway. *You're ridiculous, Darcy O'Malley. Ri-dic-u-lous.* If not so embarrassing, she'd yell the word out loud.

Their awkward moment earlier was totally her fault. She'd jokingly reached for his arm muscle, and then spazzed at the bizarre connection. She absolutely could *not* let her old crush come roaring back, or it would be impossible to work with him. Impossible to act normal around him.

"Are you sure your mom won't mind us storing

the auction items here?" Luke asked as he opened the back of her vehicle.

"There's less storage space at the church. The items will be safe here until we can set up right before the auction."

Darcy propped the front door of the house open and began to carry small items into the wood paneled study. The room still reminded her of her dad, though her mom had pretty much taken over his desk. His books still filled the shelves, and his framed photos remained on the desk.

"Is that you, Darcy?" Noreen called from the kitchen.

"Yes. We're going to unload the car."

"Dinner will be ready soon. Burt is already here."

Someone in her mom's life had put a bounce back in her step and a chronic smile on her face. Could that person actually be Burt?

As Darcy trudged back outside, Luke's cell phone rang.

He signaled for her to hold up. "Yes, I appreciate you calling me back."

He listened to the caller for another moment. "I see." Nodded. Frowned. "Yes, I understand. Please don't worry about it. We'll talk soon."

Rubbing his forehead as if trying to smooth away a headache, he tucked the phone in his pocket. "That was Mr. Haley. They aren't going to be able to donate the trip to their ski chalet after all."

"You mean they can't pay the travel expenses?"

"I mean they can't donate any of it—travel, use of the chalet or the lift tickets. We've lost the whole vacation package."

He had to be kidding. She waited for him to break into laughter and say so, but his serious expression squashed her hope.

She groaned. "That skiing package was supposed to raise the majority of our money. We've been advertising it on the church website for weeks. What happened?"

"He said unexpected financial obligations. Looks like we're going to have to knock on doors to come up with more donations, and hopefully a big one."

Which would take more of Darcy's nonexistent time. That, coupled with the strain from being around Luke, was simply too much. "I can't do this," she said under her breath as she lifted a large painting out of the car.

He grabbed hold of the frame. "I'll get that. It's too heavy."

He didn't get it. She couldn't handle the fundraiser commitment—or him. "If Chloe comes to dinner this evening, I'm going to ask her to help round up donations."

"Sure, do what you need to do." He didn't look

thrilled by the prospect as he picked up a framed mirror and headed inside.

Having another committee member still wouldn't solve the problem of Darcy handling her feelings for Luke. She'd had enough disappointment where he was concerned. She didn't need to bring more on herself.

After two more loads of items, they carried the carton holding the basketball hoop to the garage, then headed to the kitchen.

Steam rose from a boiling pot on the stove. A freshly baked pound cake sat on the granite countertop, the smell of vanilla and sweetness filling the air.

Was it Darcy's imagination, or were Burt and her mom standing awfully close? Could he be the mystery man? They looked kind of cute together and acted comfortable around each other. How could that be a bad thing? After watching her mother suffer through a year of sadness and withdrawal, followed by another year of merely getting by, Darcy liked seeing her happy.

And the affection didn't appear one-sided like Luke had suggested.

"Oh, hi, you two." Noreen's eyes were bright, her smile perky. "Now I can put the garlic bread under the broiler. It'll be ready in two minutes."

"Is Chloe coming for dinner?" Darcy asked.

Burt opened the drawer and pulled out a serving spoon. "She called to say she was running late. We're to go ahead and eat."

Darcy looked back and forth between her mom and Burt, which wasn't much of a trip. They were practically joined at the hip as they finished dinner preparations together. As if they'd cooked together many times before.

"Is something going on here?" Darcy asked before she'd had time to consider the question.

A glance at Luke, whose eyes narrowed as he took in the homey scene, showed she'd probably made an error.

"I don't know what you mean," Mom said, opening the refrigerator, staring inside.

Burt shoved his hands in his pockets and focused his attention out the window.

Neither of them would make eye contact.

Darcy chewed her lip, trying not to laugh. Something was definitely up. Then she realized the mistake of unearthing that *something* in front of Luke, who stood on the other side of the counter with hurt in his eyes.

"Yeah, Dad. Is there something you need to tell me?"

Burt squared off with his son. "Maybe there is."

"Burt." Noreen hurried over from the fridge, laid her hand on his arm and shook her head imperceptibly. The tiniest warning, so tiny Darcy almost missed it.

"We're not children," Burt said, a muscle twitching in his jaw.

Luke ran a hand through his hair. "Oh, man. This isn't one-sided. You care about her, too?"

Burt put his arm around her mother's shoulder and pulled her close beside him. "We have feelings for each other."

"Six months." Luke paced across the kitchen toward the breakfast nook. "Six measly months. Mom's barely in the grave, and her best friend and widowed husband are acting like a couple of teenagers, having *feelings* for each other."

Noreen went to him and reached out. "Please, Luke. Try to understand. We didn't mean for this to happen."

Following on Noreen's heels, Burt stopped inches from his son's face. "No need to be disrespectful," he said through gritted teeth.

"How could you? It's not decent. When word gets out, Granny will be devastated."

"This is between Noreen and me."

"This mess will involve Granny and everyone in town who knew and loved Mom."

Darcy could understand how Luke felt, but he needed to back off, to cool down before trying to discuss the situation.

She went to him and hooked her arm through his. "Come on. Let's sit down over dinner and try look at this rationally."

"Rationally? I think I'm well within reason to assume my dad wouldn't get involved with my mom's best friend so soon."

Burt took another step toward his son, his face florid.

"Don't," Noreen said, stepping between the two men, pushing them apart.

Darcy tugged on Luke's arm, pulling him toward the back door.

"What's burning?" Chloe called in a chipper voice as she popped into the kitchen from the front hall, all freshness and blonde sunshine in a room overflowing with tension…and smoke.

Mom rushed to snatch the bread out of the oven, setting off the smoke detector. As the obnoxious beeping sound rang through the kitchen, Luke stormed out the back door, slamming it behind him.

Chloe stood there, her blond silky hair perfectly smooth, in a perfectly fitted sweater set from her expensive boutique. A sweater set Darcy had admired but couldn't afford.

"Is Luke upset because I showed up?" Chloe asked, smoke from the burned bread swirling around her head as she grabbed a newspaper and fanned the blaring detector. The alarm finally shut off. Chloe gave a dainty cough.

"No, he's angry with me." Burt headed toward the door.

"Burt, wait." Noreen stepped around him to open the back door, wafting it back and forth to clear the smoke out of the room. "Maybe Darcy should go after him."

Darcy hadn't taken Luke's side on the issue and knew he would not want to see her at the moment. She let out a heavy sigh.

"I'm certainly not going after him," Chloe said in response to the sigh.

"I'll go." Darcy marched next door and let herself inside. Quietly, moving room to room, she located him in his dad's wood paneled study staring at old family photos that filled one wall.

"Are you okay?"

When he didn't answer, she stepped up behind him and put her arm around his waist.

"Don't." He shrugged her off.

Pain tweaked her chest. "I know you're mad at me, too."

"You should have backed me up. You know this isn't right."

The pain on his face made her stomach tighten into an aching knot. Why did she always hurt so badly when she knew he was hurting? "I know their relationship is way too soon. And the loss of your mom is still fresh. I totally get that."

"Then why are you so gung ho about them seeing each other when you should be discouraging it?" His eyes flashed, challenging her to do what he thought was right.

She probably should. Yet she couldn't, not when her mom was finally living again. "I can't help it if I want my mom to find someone who makes her smile. And what better man than your dad?"

Crossing his arms tightly in front of him, he stared at a large family portrait. "I'm not faulting Noreen as much as I am my dad. I think you should worry about her. There'll be talk."

"I believe their church friends will be happy for them."

He shook his head. "They'll be shocked. Maybe angry."

"No, I live around here, remember? I know these people."

This time when he tried to shake off her touch, she held tightly to his arm, trying to offer comfort.

The muscle of his forearm tensed, then relaxed. He turned to look at her. "You're being naive."

"You're being stubborn. You shut me out the moment I took Mom's and Burt's side instead of yours."

"You should side with me on this. Ending their relationship now will be best for everyone."

She huffed in disgust. "And you know what's best for everyone? No, you're just concerned you won't be able to convince your dad to move to Nashville."

Irritation flashed in his eyes. "Darcy, if you think that's all I care about, you don't know me at all."

For some reason, the comment made her throat ache. "I guess I don't anymore."

He stepped into her space, so close she caught the scent of his soap and could feel his breath tickling her bangs, so close she had to look up to meet his eyes.

"What's wrong between us?" he asked. "Something's off, and it has nothing to do with our parents."

The look in his eyes—heat, frustration, determination—sent her heart racing, her breath hitching. He was going to dig until he found out exactly what had gotten into her.

A stupid, dangerous, poorly timed attraction.

She needed to say something instead of standing there struck speechless by his nearness and the intense look in his eyes.

The powerful urge to simply pour it all out, to tell her good friend how she used to feel about him, how she feared she would feel again if she wasn't careful, pulsed in her head. If she told him, then maybe they could laugh it off and get past this awkwardness. Putting the craziness out in the open would help strengthen her resolve.

She reached up and laid her hand lightly on his chest. "Luke..."

His eyes sparked, and then he stepped away, his expression turning icy.

The rebuff sent a shock wave of cold through her body, cold enough to knock her back to her senses. What had she nearly done? She could have ruined their friendship if she'd told him.

"I don't know how we can work together on the auction with this mess with our parents," he said. "I'll tell Granny I can't do it after all."

Pain seared inside her chest. How had she been so foolish as to let old longings creep up on her again?

Lord, help me be careful.

Drawing strength from the cold dose of reality, she found the necessary words, words she should have spoken sooner. "Grace would be disappointed if you quit. I'll find someone to take my place."

Unable to look at him for fear of showing her hurt, she turned and hurried away.

What would she tell Mom and Burt and Chloe?

The truth, she supposed.

That Luke wouldn't listen to her. That he apparently didn't want to be around her at all.

Chapter Four

"You did what?"

The next day, Luke's grandmother stared at him, mouth agape, forehead wrinkled. He couldn't blame her for being angry. He already felt like a jerk for the way his conversation with Darcy had gone the previous evening, for the hurt look he'd put on her face.

Still, Darcy had quit and he needed to get his grandmother to agree to rejoin the auction committee. He had to pull together the event to help fund his mom's pet project.

"I didn't kick Darcy off," he said. "We mutually agreed it's probably not a good idea to work together right now."

Grace narrowed her eyes, and if looks could skin someone alive, he'd be a mere skeleton at the moment.

"You had to have done something. Darcy was

excited about helping the children. She'd worked hard to solicit donations. She would not up and quit."

No, she hadn't quit. He'd forced her hand.

Because something in her eyes had scared him to death. For an instant, he'd feared she might say something that would change their friendship forever. Something that could ruin it.

"Granny, what's done is done. Please, I need you to help me finish planning the auction. You know everyone who donated and can help me round up the items. Plus, the Haleys cancelled, so we need another high-bid item."

Her face fell. "No. You don't mean it. We had expected to make a bundle off that ski chalet trip. Now we won't nearly meet our increased budget."

"See why I need you?"

"I'll certainly try to find another donor. But you still need Darcy to help you pull off the auction." The confusion and frustration in her eyes turned to hurt. Her eyes filled with tears. "I simply don't understand. You and Darcy are so close. How could this happen?"

Your son-in-law went off the deep end, he wanted to say. But he didn't dare tell Granny. Not yet, anyway. If he could persuade his dad to give up the ridiculous romance with Noreen, Granny might never need to know. They could keep the relationship a secret from everyone.

Even if Burt and Noreen came to their senses, it still wouldn't change the strange attraction he'd been having to Darcy.

"Sometimes friends drift apart," he said, trying to convince himself more that Granny. "I live in another state now. We're not in contact nearly as often as in the past."

The flesh-filleting stare returned. "Instead of letting go, you should be working to rebuild your friendship. You don't just give up something so precious." She leaned closer and poked him in the chest. "In fact, I think you've taken her for granted all these years while she's been totally devoted to you. Helping you in school, tending you when you were sick or injured, cheering you on in sports, tolerating your many girlfriends."

Sure, Darcy had always been there for him, but hadn't he been there for her, too? Although, lately, she'd probably initiated more phone calls than he had.

His conscience nagged at him that he'd forgotten her birthday last year. Thankfully, he'd remembered two days later and made up for it by sending a gift.

Still, he'd forgotten. And now he'd pushed her away because of a desperate look in her eyes.

A look that, really, could have meant anything.

Maybe he'd jumped to conclusions. Maybe she'd been upset over the conflict between him and their parents. Or maybe she'd been worried about him and the pain it caused.

Pulling out his cell phone, he said, "I do need to call her. Find out if she's found a replacement yet."

"No, you need to tell her you want *her* on the committee. She's a kindhearted young woman who needs to know you value her."

His grandmother was wrong, there. Darcy knew he valued her friendship. They'd had disagreements before. They would weather this one, as well.

If Granny wouldn't help on the committee, he had to find someone. He needed to talk to Darcy.

I would if I could, Darcy.

I'm sorry, but I can't.

Sorry, but I'm learning to say no, even if it is a worthy cause.

If only you'd asked me last month.

Well, she would have asked for a volunteer last month if she'd known she'd be in this predicament.

Darcy tossed her cell phone in her purse and walked out the door of the hospital. For the past half hour, she'd heard a variety of excuses as well as direct no's. She had hit up everyone she could think of from their small congregation to take her place for the fund-raiser.

Now it was time to head to Chloe's boutique to beg her sister to take over the auction work. After the way Chloe had refused to even go after Luke yesterday during the big blowup in the kitchen, Darcy didn't hold out hope Chloe would agree. Which was why she'd saved her sister as a last resort.

Darcy parked outside Chloe's Closet, the small shop in downtown Appleton. The building stood strong, an old opera house that had been remodeled decades earlier but still held old-world charm. Chloe rented a small space for her specialty boutique that carried high-end women's clothes, gifts and items for the home. A shop Darcy had never been able to afford, even with Chloe offering items at cost.

Business for Chloe had been good, but she hadn't yet been able to afford to hire any employees. She told Darcy if she insisted on working an extra job, then when it came time to hire someone, Chloe hoped to lure Darcy away from Glenda's.

Whether she worked there or not, someday, Darcy would be able to buy cute clothes from Chloe's Closet…once she had all her loans paid off, and had bought a home.

A goal she could fully focus on now that Luke had booted her off the auction committee.

She'd looked forward to knowing her small contribution might help feed a child on the weekends during the school year. Had felt good about doing her part.

As long as Luke and the new recruit completed the work and raised enough money, then Darcy would have to be satisfied.

She sighed as she walked inside the store. Front and center sat a display stacked with patterned shorts and colorful, sleeveless knit tops. Shelves along the right-hand wall displayed everything from jewelry to candles. Photo frames and other gift items stood artfully displayed on the other wall.

"I'll be right with you," called Chloe.

Darcy ran her fingers over a gorgeous silky dress in a summery coral color. Chloe had displayed it with the perfect chunky necklace and classic leather clutch. If she wanted to better serve her own customers at the mall, Darcy should spend more time browsing here. Though Glitzy Glenda's only sold accessories, Darcy could learn from her sister. Chloe had a real knack for fashion.

A buzz sounded. She dug inside her purse and found a text message from Luke.

Have you found a replacement yet?

She huffed as she typed back, Still working on it. He sure was impatient. Finding someone to take over an event that was coming up in less than two weeks was not easy.

Her phone vibrated again, this time a call. From Luke. "Hey."

"Hey."

Silence. Awkward silence.

"So you haven't had any luck finding anyone?" he asked.

"No. I'm at Chloe's shop now to ask her."

Silence rang on the other end. "Have you tried anyone else?"

"Everyone I know. There are no takers since it's last minute. Although, one friend did offer to help the day of the auction."

Silence again. Darcy waited for several seconds, refusing to fill the space.

"We need to talk," he said.

"I can't right now. I need to talk to Chloe and then hurry to Glitzy Glenda's."

"Closing tonight?" Tension vibrated in his tone, reaching her across the line, stretching her nerves taut.

"Not that it's any of your business, but no. I get off at eight."

"That's a relief. We'll talk when you get home."

He assumed she would agree. Of course, why would he ever doubt she'd be available anytime he wanted her to be? They'd been there for each other their whole lives.

The wedge of hurt in her chest reminded her that their relationship wasn't the same after yesterday.

She had to be stronger, to protect herself. "I don't know if that'll work out. I'll text you before I leave work to let you know."

"Um, okay." Surprise tinged his voice. "If that won't work for you, then maybe we can set up something for tomorrow."

"We'll see. If all goes well with Chloe, then maybe we won't need that meeting."

Chloe waved and headed Darcy's direction.

"Gotta run," Darcy said. "I'll text you tonight."

After he told her goodbye, and they ended the call, Chloe approached looking as cute as ever. Not a single strand of her silky light blond hair was out of place. The ends, neatly trimmed at standing monthly appointments, meant split ends weren't a problem for Chloe.

Though the two of them had their share of squabbles growing up and had struggled with their relationship while Chloe dated Luke, they'd managed to grow closer in recent years.

"New dress?" Darcy asked. "I love it."

The teal linen made Chloe's eye color pop. "Yes. Came in on Friday." She twirled in a circle. "I'm glad you like it. I wasn't sure, thought maybe it made me look thick in the middle."

The straight sheath fit her like a glove, skimming in the right places to highlight her curves. Curves Darcy would kill for. "You could never look thick."

"You're so nice and slim, you don't have to worry about sheaths clinging in the wrong place."

Darcy used to think Chloe said things like that to get compliments. The older they got, the more she realized Chloe really had moments of insecurity.

Unbelievable.

"Here you go." Chloe handed Darcy an envelope. "I figured you're here to pick up the gift certificate for the auction."

"Thanks. Actually, I came because I need a big favor."

Chloe wrinkled her perky nose and groaned. "Please don't ask me to do anything at the hospital. You know the smells freak me out."

Darcy laughed, remembering the times she'd had to help Chloe outside for fresh air before she passed out. "No, this is for church. I need you to take over working on the auction committee for the Food4Kids program."

After an audible exhale of relief, Chloe smiled. "That's not as bad, but isn't the event coming up soon?"

"Two weeks."

"Why can't you finish?"

Darcy looked away and ran her finger over a nearby blouse. "Things have gotten a little tense between Luke and me. He needs someone else to help him."

A peal of laughter burst out of Chloe. "You've got to be kidding. Can you really see Luke and me working together?"

No, Darcy couldn't. That didn't change the fact Luke needed someone. Anyone. "You two will do fine when you're working toward a goal. And you'll be an asset because you know local business owners. You can round up more donations, which we desperately need after losing the ski trip."

Chloe waved off the suggestion. "No. You and Luke just need to work out your differences. You're never mad at each other for more than five minutes."

Only this time, the problem was different. They weren't having a squabble over what movie to see or where to go for college spring break. "This is bigger. He's furious about Mom and Burt seeing each other."

Chloe's silvery blue eyes lit up. "I was dying to talk to you about it last night, but didn't think I could say much with Mom and Burt around. I'm so excited for them."

"Yeah, I'm happy, too. Obviously, Luke isn't. We argued."

Chloe rolled her eyes and tsked. "You'll make up before the day is over. I mean, seriously, you two should go ahead and marry each other. I don't know how you'll ever wed other people. Your poor spouses would have to share you too much."

Darcy's stomach plunged. Her cheeks scorched as if someone had lit them with a blowtorch. "Maybe if we felt that way about each other, but we don't. We've never been anything more than friends."

One perfectly shaped brow arched higher than the other. "Absolutely no attraction? For real?"

"Never." If you didn't count the odd connection they'd had the past few days. Which, she was sure, was one-sided.

And if you didn't count the major crush she had on him in high school. And college.

"I think you two need to rethink your relationship."

"That's what we're doing. Like you said, it's probably time to let it go. To prepare for moving on with our lives."

Chloe shook her head as she waved and walked away. "That's not what I said. But you believe what you need to believe. Now, I've got to finish a display of these great new handbags." She lifted a large tote out of a box. "You need to get one of these now. They'll be all the rage in the fall."

Ignoring her sister's sudden change of topic, Darcy jammed her hands on her hips and huffed. "Are you sure you can't help Luke?"

"I'm positive," she called with her back to Darcy while arranging the new bags. "I'm too busy right now."

And Darcy wasn't busy?

She honestly had no one else to ask to replace her on the auction committee. She'd have to meet with Luke tonight to inform him, and to find out what he was going to do about it.

Getting the brush-off was no fun. Especially when it was from his own father.

Luke had spent the entire day at home, catching up on work and dealing with the roofers, assuming his dad would show up at some point. But it was eight-thirty in the evening, and Burt hadn't made contact all day. He'd apparently gone to the office extremely early and had stayed for the duration. Clearly avoiding Luke.

If Luke stood any chance of getting his dad to move to Nashville, and thus ending the relationship with Noreen, he needed to try to make peace with him. The two of them needed to work on a plan to honor his mother at the auction.

Luke also wanted to run an auction donation idea past him, so he called his dad's cell phone.

"What can I do for you, Luke?"

At least he took my call. "I wondered if you'd be home for a late dinner."

"No, I ate at Noreen's. Will be here a little longer."

Luke's stomach growled as he nestled the phone against his shoulder and opened the refrigerator.

"Okay. I'd like to call a truce and talk when you get home. Also wanted to see if you and Noreen might donate a week at the lake house for the auction."

His dad hesitated. "So you're acknowledging we're a couple?"

Luke ground his teeth together. "I'm asking since you're co-owners. We've had a major donation fall through, and I thought y'all might agree to help."

A woman spoke in the background before the sound was muffled. The two of them held an indecipherable discussion, muted by a hand.

"Luke, dear, this is Noreen," she said a moment later. "Why don't you come over and eat? We have plenty of leftovers. And you can tell us about your idea for the lake house getaway."

Apparently, she'd commandeered the phone. He could imagine how that conversation had gone. His dad would not be pleased at the moment.

Luke had hoped to have a private conversation with his father. Now, that wouldn't be possible.

"Thanks. I'll be right over."

By the time he'd walked out his door and stuck his head inside Noreen's back door, she had made a plate of food and popped it into the microwave.

"Come on in," Noreen said, all smiles, the quintessential hostess. She'd always made him feel welcome, offering their house as his second home.

And now, even after the way he'd behaved yesterday, she acted as if nothing was amiss.

He felt bad, but it didn't change his opinion of their relationship. "Thanks. I appreciate the dinner."

Luke glanced over at his dad, who sat stoically at the table as if Noreen had threatened him to act civil. Luke nodded his head. "Dad."

"I saw the roofers came today."

"They did. They finished the back. Will finish the front tomorrow."

"Does it look good?"

"Yes, sir. They're doing a fine job. Hard workers."

The microwave dinged, and Noreen directed him to the table across from Burt.

"Thanks."

She set a plate of delicious lasagna in front of him.

Luke explained the loss of the ski chalet vacation package while intermittently blowing on his food to cool the gooey cheese on top. "So, would you two be willing to donate the use of the lake house for a week?"

Burt, his eyes serious, nodded. "We would. Especially if it'll honor your mother and help the kids she so loved."

"I appreciate it."

"There's one condition, though," Noreen said.

"We'll need you and Darcy to drive up and open the house for the season. We won't get a chance to go before July."

That job would fall on him now. "Sure. I'll be glad to do that."

She set a glass of sweet iced tea in front of him and joined them at the table. "The problem will be finding a time when Darcy can get away for a day."

"I can do it. No problem."

"Think how fun it would be for the two of you to spend some time together at the lake," she said.

How could he explain that they wouldn't be spending any more time together? At least not until they worked out their differences. If he'd overreacted yesterday, he owed her an apology.

Noreen leaned closer and put her hand on Luke's arm. "I'm worried about her. She seemed stressed last night and this morning, was poring over financial paperwork and then mentioned she wanted to give me more privacy. I'm sure it's over the fact that Burt and I are seeing each other."

"She could probably use some reassurance," he said, recalling Darcy's worries and the drive to pay off the student loans. And now he'd added to her stress over the auction.

"She needs you, Luke. At least while you're home," Noreen said.

"I'll check on her."

Relief flooded Noreen's face. "Oh, good. I feel better knowing you'll look out for Darcy, like always."

"Did I hear my name?" Darcy stood in the doorway. When she spotted Luke at the table, her eyes widened. "Oh, I didn't realize we had company."

"Not company," Noreen said with a laugh. "Burt and Luke."

"Hey, Darcy," Luke said. "Your mom was nice enough to invite me for some of her amazing lasagna."

He hadn't seen Darcy since yesterday, and she looked strained. Tired. Worry put a little crinkle between her eyebrows. He hated that he'd put it there.

"I texted you. Was planning on heading over to your house once I changed clothes," she said.

"Oh?" her mom asked. "Are you two going out?"

Darcy's gaze darted to his, as if to question how much their parents knew. "Um, no. We're discussing the auction."

"I'm so pleased that you two are working to honor Joan," Burt said. "She would be proud."

"Actually, I've handed the reins over to Luke. We were going to meet tonight to discuss the transition."

"Why?" asked Noreen.

"I'm too busy," she said, giving the most likely excuse.

"You loved working on that project," Burt said.

"I just don't have a moment to spare right now."

Noreen, who'd always been very perceptive, the mother who was never fooled, slid her attention from Darcy to Luke and back. "You were doing fine before Sunday. There's more going on here."

"Actually, there is." Luke ignored Darcy's scowl, opting to reveal the full truth—or rather the version of the truth that involved their parents. "We've found it difficult to work together after the disagreement yesterday. We were going to meet this evening to discuss Darcy's replacement."

Burt stood and leaned his fists on the table. "That's ridiculous. You can't let my relationship with Noreen—which is our business—stand in the way of a charitable project."

Darcy sighed. "You're not standing in the way. Luke will do a fine job carrying out the fundraiser."

"He needs your help, Darcy." Noreen blinked tears from her eyes. "Besides, you can't let us spoil your lifelong friendship."

"I'm afraid your relationship will ruin yours and Dad's longtime friendship," Luke said.

Burt raked a hand through his hair. "Luke, I thought you came here tonight to talk, make peace."

"I did, but I hoped you'd see reason."

Burt shook his head, disappointed. "Noreen, thanks for dinner, for trying to fix this." He backed away from the table.

She hopped up, stopping him. "Stay. We need to work this out."

"I do want to make peace," Luke said. "But I won't stand by and watch you hurt Granny."

"And you think Darcy quitting the auction committee won't hurt Grace?"

Though Burt had a point, Luke wouldn't back down on his stance over the inappropriate relationship. "Look, I know you two care about each other." He turned to his dad. "Noreen is amazing, has always been like a second mom to—" He cleared his throat, took a breath. "It's too soon, Dad. I'm afraid you're not ready, might not know what you want or need."

"Son—" Burt huffed out a breath and stared at the ceiling, trying to control his emotions.

They were both too raw to have this conversation. "Darcy and I need to talk. Privately."

"How about out back?" Wide-eyed, Darcy opened the door, motioning him outside.

He stared at his dad a moment longer. "I haven't told Granny anything yet. It's not too late to end the relationship before she finds out. And then later, if you still feel the same, maybe—"

"Noreen and I aren't ending anything."

Staring into his dad's determined eyes, Luke realized Burt was serious about not backing down. Luke's gut clenched, and frustration zipped through his veins. "Then you need to tell Granny."

Burt crossed his arms. "This is no one's business but our own. I'll tell her when we're ready to go out in public together."

"If you can't be seen in public together, don't you think that's an indication it's too soon?"

Something flashed in Burt's eyes, but he didn't retreat.

Luke shook his head. "I'd like permission to tell her now, before she accidentally finds out."

"Fine."

Luke hated the look of hurt on Noreen's face. "Noreen, are you okay with me telling Granny?"

She nodded and gave him a gentle smile. "I want to do whatever makes you most comfortable."

A soft hand took hold of his. "Come on," Darcy said.

How had Luke's life turned into this mess? His father wouldn't move to Nashville with Noreen in the picture. Clients had already left the firm where he'd invested his life savings in a mortgage and others might follow. He and Darcy were at odds. Even Granny was upset with him.

And now he'd have to go tell this news to Granny.

Darcy led him outside, her hand a comfort when everything around him seemed to have fallen apart.

Chapter Five

"I can't believe Dad won't listen to what I'm trying to tell him," Luke said as he dropped into the metal two-person seat.

The old-fashioned patio glider, white with lime-green trim, was probably as old as Darcy and had rested on the far side of their back patio as long as she could remember. The outside lights were off, so she and Luke sat bathed in moonlight.

With one leg folded underneath her, Darcy angled to face him. "Your dad can't believe *you* won't listen to *him*."

"I just can't deal with this, with him having feelings for someone besides my mom. Even if it is someone as nice as your mom." Luke let his head fall backward and groaned.

"Ah, I see. So you'd rather him still be at home, depressed and despondent."

When he looked up, she grinned, trying to defuse the situation with humor.

"You can be irritating, you know," he said, lifting one corner of his mouth in what promised to be a smile.

"Yeah, one of my many talents."

She wanted to take his hand again, to reassure him. With the way she'd been feeling lately, she couldn't. Whenever he touched her, things got dicey.

Time to talk about the auction. "I couldn't find anyone to join you on the committee. I'm sorry."

"Granny said she'd search for another donor, but claimed she couldn't help otherwise."

Darcy pushed with her foot, setting the glider in motion. "Maybe you can manage. At this point, you're mainly picking up donations."

"And trying to find the big replacement. Our parents have donated a week at the lake house, but it's not going to bring in nearly what the ski trip would have. Any suggestions?"

She shook her head. "We hit up everyone already. What about someone in Nashville? Or do you know anyone in Atlanta?"

"I'll think on it."

How had everything gotten so complicated?

As they sat side by side on the glider on which they'd spent many hours of their life, all the strange feelings she'd been sensing between them seemed silly.

This was Luke. Her best friend. Sitting beside her in the spot he'd always held, talking out problems like they'd always done.

Luke rested his arm along the back of the seat, not quite touching her. She could feel the heat radiating from his skin.

"Will you please work with me on the auction?" he asked, looking surprised, as if he hadn't thought through the request before speaking.

Though her heart raced, she guarded against revealing her own surprise. "Feeling desperate?"

"Actually, no. Though, granted, I want to make the event successful."

"Then why?"

"Because I made a mistake in saying we shouldn't work together."

Luke Jordan didn't apologize often, and she would milk this one for all it was worth. "Oooh, the attorney admits to the jury he was wrong."

His mouth inched up into a half smile. "Yeah. There's a first for everything, huh?"

"So why the change of heart?"

"Because we're friends. No matter what our parents do. No matter how weird it—" He stopped midsentence, and something sparked in his eyes.

"Weird?" The moonlight reflected off his eyes as she held his gaze. The glider stilled.

With the hand lying along the back of the seat, he reached out, pushed her hair over her shoulder, a gesture he'd done many times over the years. Only this time, he lingered as he rubbed her hair between his fingers.

She drew in a deep, controlled breath, then slowly leaned away, sliding away from his grasp. She had to be careful.

As if he sensed her discomfort, he crossed his arms over his chest. "We're friends. No matter how weird our parents are acting."

Oh, okay. So they were back to talking about their parents. Probably a good thing. A safer topic than other strange feelings she feared he would bring up.

"I do hate leaving you in the lurch," she said.

"Then let's forget what we said yesterday. Work with me on this. Dad and Noreen need us to open the lake house for the season. If you can manage to get off work and go with me, maybe we can have a little fun with the cleaning."

She sagged in relief, and once again sent the glider into motion with the push of her foot. "Okay. I'll help you."

"Will you also go with me to tell Granny about Dad and your mom?"

His concern for Graced touched her. "Why me?"

"I think when you see how it affects her, you'll change your mind about our parents."

She widened her eyes at him. "And then take your side?"

He laughed as he stood, pulled her to her feet and wrapped her in a friendly hug. "It's good to be home, to be here with you."

With initial contact, she stiffened but almost immediately relaxed and slipped her arms around his waist. If they were going to work together, she would have to chill. Would have to act like she always had. "It's good to have my friend back."

Yeah, she'd been a fool. All was well with Luke, everything back to normal. To help hungry kids, she could manage working with him without getting hurt.

The next afternoon, Luke followed Darcy up his grandmother's front steps, placed his hand on her lower back and reached around to tap on the door. "We have to break the news about our parents gently."

This was the moment. The moment when Darcy would see she was wrong about their parents, would change her mind. And, yes, as she said last night, would take his side.

She glanced at him, wariness in her eyes. From his touch?

Yeah, he was probably standing too close. But she smelled so good, and they'd always shared space as if it wasn't anything.

Apparently, they couldn't anymore.

He clenched his teeth, wanting to rail against the frustration. "I thought we were good. Have I done something else to offend you that you're not telling me about?"

"No." Her gaze darted over his shoulder. A tell. She was not being truthful.

The door opened, and his grandmother stood grinning behind the screen. "What a nice surprise. Can I safely assume you two are working together again?" Grace ushered Darcy and Luke inside and led them to the kitchen, the heart of Granny's house—the heart of Luke's family.

"We are, Granny," Luke said, pleased that she was happy with him once again.

They sat in their regular places around her table. How many meals had they shared through the years? Granny, his dad, his mom and even Darcy.

"How about some coffee or pie?"

"No, thanks." Darcy smiled at Granny as if all was well in her world. "We only have a few minutes before I need to head to the mall to work."

Apparently, Darcy still assumed their visit wouldn't affect his grandmother. He turned to Grace, took her soft hand in his. "We need to talk with you, Granny, about something upsetting."

The corners of her mouth drew downward. Concern deepened the crease between her brows as she looked from one of them to the other.

He didn't even know how to begin.

With a tilt of her head, Darcy flashed him an irritated look.

"What is it, son?"

"I have some news about Dad."

Grace's hand shot to her chest as she gasped.

"No, it's nothing bad," Darcy said. "Burt's fine. Luke thought you should know that—"

"That Dad is, uh, seeing someone," Luke finished.

"Seeing someone? As in dating?"

Luke swallowed hard as he nodded, waiting for Granny to fall apart.

Grace huffed and slouched in her chair, as if all the starch had gone out of her. "My goodness. You nearly scared me to death. Why didn't you say that to start with?"

Darcy let out a sigh and shook her head yet refrained from saying "I told you so."

"Don't you think it's way too soon?" Luke said. "I mean, I thought you'd be upset."

Granny considered the question as she rubbed one thumb over the other. "Granted, this has come about rather quickly, but men sometimes do that. Everyone grieves differently."

"I'm afraid there's more to the story."

She raised her chin, waiting.

"The woman he has feelings for is…well, it's Noreen."

His grandmother sat motionless. "You don't say." She glanced at Darcy. "Did you know about this?"

"I suspected she had a man in her life. I didn't know it was Burt until this past Sunday when we all got together for dinner. What about you, did you have an inkling?"

"I've seen it coming, probably before either of them did."

Luke's breath hissed through his teeth. "Then why didn't you say something, *do* something to stop what's sure to be a train wreck?"

She gripped his hand and squeezed. "Don't begrudge him this. Your dad loved your mother and never wavered over the last horrible, awful two years of her life. He was there for her every step of the way. He deserves to find happiness."

Unable to sit a moment longer, Luke popped up and paced the length of the kitchen.

"Come on, Luke," Darcy said. "You can't change their feelings. Let them be. They'll figure out the relationship."

"Six months. Six lousy months." He pushed his hand through his hair, then glanced at Darcy. "When my phone buzzes on a Wednesday morning, I still expect it's her weekly call. When I check email, I'm still surprised not to see her name in my in-box."

The distressed expression on Darcy's face

nearly undid him. She came over and wrapped her arms around him, forcing him to swallow the grief pushing at his throat before he made a fool of himself.

"I'm so sorry," she said, laying her head against his chest.

"It's too soon for Dad to think he cares about someone else."

"I know. I'm sorry if I've pushed you to accept this."

Relaxing into her, he rested his cheek on the top of her head, breathing in the familiar clean smell of her hair, allowing her to share the pain that had been lashing at him since Sunday evening.

How had he survived law school and months of living in Nashville without her?

"Luke, honey, I'm sorry you're hurting," Grace said. "But I think we need to stay out of their business and let them find their way."

Pulling away from Darcy, Luke took a slow breath and placed a hand on Granny's shoulder. "The townspeople will be shocked. Mom's friends may be angry and say something to hurt Dad or Noreen...or you."

"Let them talk. The relationship is none of *their* business, either."

Luke didn't agree. "I won't stand by while they dishonor Mom's memory."

Darcy tensed. "While who dishonors her memory—the townspeople or our parents?"

"Both."

No matter what Darcy and his grandmother thought, Luke was determined to stop his dad from seeing Noreen.

If Darcy wouldn't help him talk sense into their parents, then maybe Chloe could help.

He didn't like the thought of approaching her, but he had to do *something.*

Despite any awkwardness, he had to try and win Chloe over to his side.

"What a sneaky, underhanded thing to do."

Darcy stood outside the locked door of Chloe's Closet Thursday evening with a rare evening off work and glanced at the text her sister had sent. A message informing her she couldn't get together for dinner because Luke had pestered her for two days until she had agreed to meet him at the café to discuss their parents. Chloe's next message told Darcy not to worry, she planned to tell him exactly how she felt about his interference.

Mr. Persistent hadn't been able to persuade Darcy to join the breakup posse, so he was going to secretly try to woo Chloe to his side. *Good luck with that.* Thinking of Chloe telling him off left a smile on Darcy's face.

Even though Darcy knew Luke didn't stand a

chance of making headway with Chloe, she strode toward the café, a half block off the downtown square on McIntosh Road.

Though she had no intention of making a scene, she would crash Luke's little party. She needed to make sure he didn't do anything to hurt her mom.

At the entrance of the café, she smoothed her hand over the front of her blouse and tightened her ponytail, taking time to gather herself.

Stepping inside, she breathed in the aroma of fried chicken and scanned the crowded dining room. Chloe and Luke weren't immediately visible.

The café waitress-owner Edna, a short middle-aged woman with stylish salt-and-pepper hair and the deepest of Southern accents, paused with an armload of plates of steaming food lined up her arm. "Hi, darlin'. Haven't seen you in ages."

"I've barely had time to eat lately."

"Oh, sugar, I totally understand. Have a seat anywhere."

"Actually, I'm looking for my sister."

Edna nodded toward the back corner. "Over there." She leaned in close enough for Darcy to smell the bacon on a club sandwich. "So, are Chloe and your buddy Luke dating again?"

Dating?

Darcy's heart sank. Were the two of them holding hands or something? Was this dinner more than she'd thought?

"I don't think so, Edna." She pulled the corners of her lips upward, even though she wanted to do anything but smile.

Dreading what she'd discover, she meandered between tables of the packed restaurant, chatting with three families from church celebrating five-year-old Charlie's birthday, two tellers from the bank and the ladies from the hair salon having a going-away dinner for one of the new stylists who was moving to Atlanta.

"Hey, girl," said her longtime hairstylist, Norma. "I see Luke is home. Guess you're heading his way."

Darcy nodded. "I'm glad to have him back for a visit."

Norma cupped her hands to whisper. "So, are he and Chloe an item again?"

"Not that I know of."

"Oh, they make such a cute couple. I hope they're back together."

Darcy stamped on another tense smile, wished the young stylist who was moving a happy life, and finally made her way to the booth in the back. She was met with Chloe's laugh. Darcy's chest squeezed, making it hard to breathe.

Inching closer, she stepped in sight of the table.

Luke spotted her first. His jaw twitched like it always did when he was frustrated.

Chloe turned to see what had drawn Luke's attention. "Oh, hey, Darcy. Come join us." She scooted over to make room, as if nothing was going on, as if being interrupted wasn't a big deal.

Darcy was being ridiculous. Even if Luke and Chloe decided to date again, she had no right to be upset.

"Thanks." She slid in beside her sister, refocusing her thoughts on Luke and his apparent plan. "So, what's up? Is Luke trying to pull you onto his team in the battle for the parents?"

Chloe laughed at the same time Norma said something about purple hair that sent the table of hair stylists into a fit of giggles.

"You do know Luke well," Chloe said.

Darcy glared at the guilty party. "I knew something was up since the two of you haven't gotten together willingly since college."

Luke relaxed in the booth with his arms resting along the back of the seat. "I merely wanted to talk to Chloe about our parents. To see if she has any insight into the relationship."

"So, do you, Chloe?" Darcy asked.

She shrugged. "I told Luke I don't know any more than either of you. I have to say, I'm happy for Mom. She's like a new person the past few weeks."

Darcy wanted to nod in her best I-told-you-so manner, but she knew Luke was hurting, and that she should have more compassion. She wasn't going to push him to accept their parents dating, would let him deal with it however he needed.

As long as he didn't sabotage her mother's happiness.

"I told Luke I think we need to stay out of it," Darcy said.

"I told him the same thing." Chloe leaned her chin on her hand and watched Luke as if waiting for his response.

Someone at the next table gasped.

"Oh, my stars," Norma said.

"Will you look at that?" The raspy voice belonged to Shirley from the salon.

Luke leaned to peer around the edge of the booth. His eyes fell closed, and he let out an exasperated sigh. "You've got to be kidding."

Darcy craned her neck to see what had the café buzzing.

Noreen and Burt stood inside the door.

Holding hands.

The chatter and clang of silverware in the small diner faded away and, other than noise in the kitchen, all grew quiet.

"What is it?" Chloe asked.

"Mom and Burt. Obviously together."

Chloe gave Darcy a little push. "Don't just stare. Go ask if they want to join us."

Darcy stood but then turned back to Luke. “They’d be pleased if you invited them.”

Red streaked his cheeks. “I won’t do anything rude if you invite them over.”

In other words, he didn’t want to do anything to condone the relationship.

“Come on, Luke. Your dad deserves a life,” Chloe said.

“That’s okay. Never mind.” Darcy headed toward their parents as Edna showed them to a table for two along the far wall.

Every single person in the café stared at the couple. A few wore tense smiles. One brave soul, Norma, waved and greeted them while the majority looked on with frowns or expressions of downright disapproval.

Darcy’s gaze flew to her mother, who appeared to be holding on to Burt’s hand like a vise. Noreen smiled, nodding and waving to friends as they moved to their table, her face suffused in red, yet head held high.

Burt didn’t handle the attention as well. He stared straight ahead, mouth drawn.

Hurting for both of them, Darcy rushed over as they were about to sit. “Hey. Do y’all want to join Chloe, Luke and me in the back booth?”

Her mom gave an appreciative smile. Then she glanced around the room. “Um, thank you. But we're fine here. Having our first public date," she whispered.

"I gathered that."

"I can feel the disapproval. This is none of their business," Burt said through clenched teeth.

Noreen rubbed his hand, smoothing over the white-knuckled fist. "They're surprised. They'll adjust."

He zoomed his attention to Noreen, his gaze softening, and gently rubbed his thumb over hers. "They're judging me, and I hate how it's reflecting on you, making you feel bad."

Mom looked up. "Darcy, honey, thank you for braving coming over here. Thank Luke, too, because I know he's probably upset by this whole scene."

"I will. Hope you have nice dinner."

As she wove her way back to the table, she heard snippets of conversation that included the names Noreen, Burt, Grace...and Joan.

Their parents had set the whole place abuzz.

Her poor mother. She looked mortified, wounded. These were her friends—people from the church, the salon and the bank. People Mom dealt with on a daily basis. People who should be happy for her.

Yet not a single one acted as if they approved of the relationship.

Chloe came barreling toward Darcy, then

stopped in the middle of the café and jammed her hands on her hips, taking a moment to stare at each table around the room. "Goodness, Edna," she called loud enough for everyone to hear. "I thought this place was usually filled with the kindest, most welcoming people in Appleton." Said in her sweetest Southern drawl, the words shamed the customers so nicely they probably wanted to thank her for it.

Proud, and wishing she had the same gumption, Darcy bit back a grin and gave her sister's arm a quick squeeze.

"Where are y'all's manners?" Edna barked. "Now, let these folks eat in peace. We need to sing 'Happy Birthday' to little Charlie."

As the guilty-faced diners sang to the five-year-old, Chloe pointed to the door and mouthed "I'm leaving." Darcy waved to her sister and returned to the table where Luke waited. The song ended, and the diners resumed normal conversation.

Luke grimaced and rubbed his temples. "This is exactly the kind of scene I'd hoped to avoid."

"I know. Maybe the worst is over." Darcy couldn't help worrying about her mom, though. What if Luke was right?

Maybe she should have discouraged the relationship to protect Noreen. If things got messy, it could ruin a lifelong family friendship, even destroy some long-term friendships with townspeople.

She better keep that in mind with her feelings for Luke, too. Time to be realistic. Time to buckle down and concentrate only on the auction.

"We need to get together to finalize the newspaper ad," she said. "Deadline is Monday at noon."

He dragged his gaze away from their parents, and the scowl eased. "How does tomorrow look?"

"I work the early shift at the hospital, so I'll have a couple of hours before I head to the mall at five."

"I'll drop by at three. We can pick up a few more auction items and then work on the ad."

She saluted. "Yes, sir."

The rest of the tension eased from his face. He leaned across the table, so close she could see the little flecks of dark brown in his golden-brown eyes. "I am *not* trying to be bossy."

She leaned in as well, forearms resting on the table. "You are acting bossy. Like usual."

"I'm decisive."

"Uh-huh. You can think that if you want."

They were nearly nose to nose, both grinning. His fingertips brushed her hand. Then he threaded his fingers through first one hand, then the other, palm to palm, like they used to do when they'd play Mercy—which he always won. This time, though, he didn't twist his wrists trying to get her to call out for mercy. No, he simply held on to her, dragging his attention from her face to their joined hands, his expression growing serious.

"So, Miss O'Malley," he said, "would three o'clock tomorrow be convenient for you to get together to work on the auction?"

When he looked back into her eyes with a sweet smile curving his lips, one side a little higher than the other, she had the sudden urge to cry. Instead, out of the touch-induced foggy-headedness, she dredged up their mantra. *Remember Chloe.*

Luke was good at this. This charming, make you swoon act. He used it on all the girls. Hadn't she witnessed it many times over? He charmed them, won them over, then moved on to the next.

She took a deep breath and smiled. Pulled her fingers from his and tucked them in her lap. "Why, that's very kind of you, sir. I think that would be convenient."

He leaned back in the booth, looking almost relieved. "Good. It's a date."

The word *date* gave her a start, a word she used to dream about hearing form his lips. "Yeah, it's a date. To work," she reminded.

He smiled, although it wasn't one of his goofy, typical smiles. "Of course that's what I meant." He stood and laid cash on the table. "I'll see you tomorrow, Darcy."

At least they both now knew where they stood. No nose-to-nose grinning. No hand-holding.

No calling their time together a date. Thankfully, they were nothing like their parents.

Then why did she feel so disheartened?

Chapter Six

She's totally aloof.

Luke stuck his head in the door and peered across the backseat of his car, over the top of a box, as Darcy grabbed a bag full of donated yarn they'd picked up. Maybe she was just tired from working the early shift at the hospital that morning.

"We've collected almost everything on our list," he said.

She met his eyes with the same distant expression she'd worn all afternoon as they'd driven around to multiple homes and stores.

Or maybe she was simply focused on the business at hand. Which was what he needed to do to make this the best fund-raiser ever.

"We still need to clean and ready the lake house in case the winning bidder wants it immediately," she said.

"I have a lot more free time on my hands. I can do it this weekend."

She hefted the unopened bag of yarn—donated by a young woman at the church who'd found it stored in her mother's home after the woman's death. "Or I can help…if you want."

"Don't you work this weekend?"

"I'm off at the hospital Saturday. My coworker, a single mom, needed the extra hours."

Typical bighearted Darcy. Even though she herself was trying to earn every penny she could, she'd given up her hours to help someone else. "So you could go with me Saturday morning?"

She nodded. "I'd need to be back in time to work at Glenda's that evening."

"Sounds like a plan, then. How about we leave at ten? I've arranged breakfast with Dad that morning."

"To talk to him about moving to Tennessee?"

Hopefully. But only if Luke felt the timing was right. "Not sure yet, but that's the plan."

Standing on one foot and kicking the car door closed with the other, she stumbled backward into him. He set her upright.

"I thought that was the whole reason you were here," she said.

"His dating your mom has changed the situation."

She gave him an apologetic look as they hauled the last of the donations to her dad's office.

With hands resting on her hips, she blew hair off her forehead and surveyed the crowded room. "What next? I have about five minutes to spare."

"We need to look at the newspaper ad," he said. "And round up something significant to put *in* the ad."

She opened a laptop computer and pulled up a file on the screen. "This is what I've designed so far."

"Looks good to me. Except for the big gaping hole where the ski trip used to be."

With a sigh, she plopped into her dad's office chair. "Too bad we don't know someone filthy rich or famous."

He rubbed his chin and grimaced. "Haven't we launched anyone out of Appleton who's really successful?"

Darcy gasped. Popped straight out of the chair. "We have. I can't believe I didn't think of him sooner!"

"Who?"

"Well, he's not really famous yet. He's been making it big on the music scene in Atlanta and is now causing a little stir in Nashville."

"Country music?"

"Yeah. Bryan Winningham. The drummer in our high school band." She raised her brows as if she expected him to recognize the name.

Luke couldn't remember him. When he didn't show any signs of recognition, she rolled her eyes.

"I'm sorry. Must not have had any classes with him."

"Of course you did. You were too busy breaking girls' hearts to notice a sweet, quiet guy in the marching band." Shaking her head, she shut the laptop. "I need to get ready for work. We can finish the ad this weekend once I've had a chance to contact him."

Luke experienced an odd sense of dissonance to find out Darcy had a friend he never knew about. Was there more to it and she'd never told him? Had she had a crush on the guy? "So you know him well enough to call?"

"Yeah. We talked a few times over the summers during college, have kept in touch by phone off and on since then. I should still have his number. And if not, I'll get it from his parents." She smiled and shooed him toward the door. "I need to change clothes. I'll see you tomorrow morning at ten."

He didn't want to say goodbye yet. "I'll drive you to the mall."

"If you do that, you'll have to pick me up later."

He shrugged. "No problem. What time?"

She headed out of the office and toward the

stairs. "You don't have to play guard dog. I'm not closing tonight."

He would leave no room for argument. "What time?"

"Fine. Nine o'clock." She hurried up the stairs toward her bedroom.

Why was it always so rewarding to irritate her? He smiled as he went to wait in the car then honked the horn to rush her, just for good measure.

Yet the smile faded as he wondered once again about this Bryan Winningham.

By the time she slid into the passenger seat, he thought maybe he recalled the drummer. "So this Bryan guy. Did he have shaggy brown hair that always hung in his eyes?"

"You mean like yours in high school?" she snapped. "The hair that made all the girls want to push it out of your eyes?"

A laugh burst out of him. "*All* the girls?" he couldn't help teasing.

"Not this girl," she said, pointing a thumb at her chest. "But, yes, he had the same hair."

"So you never wanted to push Bryan's hair back for him?" He said it in a joking voice, but for some crazy reason, he needed to know.

"Of course not. Like I said, he was sweet. And really shy. A lot of kids made fun of him for being nerdy. Which I could empathize with."

The friendship suddenly made perfect sense. "So you took him under your wing."

She buckled her seat belt. "Not really. We bonded over shared misery."

Why had he never known about this other friendship? Had he been so clueless and into his own life that he hadn't noticed?

Worse, why did the thought of Darcy having a crush on someone bother him so much?

"Luke, we really need to go, or I'll be late."

On the way to the mall, they brainstormed potential donation items, in case Bryan didn't work out. They still couldn't come up with anything that would bring in the amount the Colorado ski trip could have brought in.

"Thanks for the ride," Darcy said as he pulled into a parking space.

"I'm coming in. Might get something for Granny." He hurried around to open her door for her.

"Thanks. Yeah, Grace is always dressed to the nines. She puts my wardrobe to shame."

He glanced at her midcalf-length khaki pants—capris or whatever they were called. Her brown polo shirt. And brown leather sandals. "Is that a uniform?"

She laughed as she bumped her shoulder into his. "No, you goof. This is an example of the terrible wardrobe I was telling you about."

"You looked nice at church this past Sunday in that skirt."

Her face turned a nice shade of pink, the blush highlighting her fair, freckled skin. "I'm surprised you even noticed."

"Of course I'd notice if you wore a dress or skirt. Isn't that like a once-in-a-century event?" He winked at her as he opened the door into the mall.

"You're hard on a girl's ego."

"I'm speaking the truth. I never understood why you refused girly clothes."

"I don't have curves like Chloe. I fit better into tailored outfits."

He wasn't touching that comment. She tended to get sensitive and never believed him when he said she had a nice figure. He'd given up years ago.

Instead, he glanced at his watch as they reached the store. "I got you here right on time."

She met his eyes, and he thought he saw hurt there. "Thanks. I'll see you at nine."

She headed through the doorway to clock in on the cash register.

He'd blown it again. Like usual. Yet they'd always managed to push past his blunders.

Joining her inside, he glanced around the store, overwhelmed by jewelry, purses and other…stuff. What on earth would his grandmother like?

A group of three young teen girls walked in.

One was louder than the others and obviously in charge. She whispered something to one of the other girls, and then laughed. The third one, a redhead, looked upset, as if she knew the others were making fun of her.

Oh, boy. Exactly the scenario Darcy had been talking about. As Darcy passed him, moving toward the customers, he circled his hand around her wrist to slow her. "I'm sorry."

"For what?"

"For being a jerk. For saying the wrong things, and hurting your feelings about your clothes."

"It's not your fault. It's just one of my hang-ups."

"Um, *excuse me,*" said one of the girls in a snarky tone that made him want to tell her to watch her manners. "How much is this tacky purse? My friend wants to know."

"This is your chance to make that sale," he whispered with a wink before squeezing her hand and then letting go.

"Actually, your friend has great taste," Darcy said to the girl while holding his gaze. Her smile whopped him in the gut as she walked toward the customer. "Let's go look up the price. I believe it's on sale today."

Luke left the store, his chest tight. And realized halfway to the car that he hadn't bought his grandmother a single thing.

* * *

Emboldened by Luke's comment, Darcy scanned the shop and discovered that the girl who liked the so-called tacky purse was the redhead from the other night, the one who'd left the pink pearls behind. The rude, mouthy one was the same ringleader.

"Come on over here," Darcy called to the redhead. "This fantastic bag is on sale."

The girl's expression lifted, as if having someone affirm her taste had worked wonders.

Mean Girl rolled her eyes. "Don't encourage her."

The third girl snickered.

Something inside Darcy snapped. She'd been this girl before, the one left out, the one teased.

Darcy turned her back to the rude one and focused her attention on the redhead. She pointed to the sale sign. "The purses on this table are fifty percent off. Cute bag, all the rage, nice deal."

She handed it to the timid girl, whose eyes darted to her friends.

"You won't look right carrying a bag that big," Mean Girl said. "It looks like a mom purse."

"All the celebrities are carrying them," Darcy said, smiling to encourage the girl. "I bet the girls at your school are behind on the style." Thanks to Chloe's shop display, Darcy knew the trend was hitting the Atlanta area.

"Come on. The movie starts soon," the leader said. "We don't have time to listen to this chick spout off something she doesn't know anything about. This is some cheap chain store." She grabbed the snickering girl's arm and headed out of the shop, leaving the redhead behind.

Looking apologetic, the girl stood holding her bag, trying to decide whether or not to follow her friend out the door.

Darcy took the bag from her and set it back on the table. "Listen, I'm not trying to make a sale. I've been in your shoes before. Don't let her boss you around."

"She can make my life miserable."

"Isn't she already?"

The girl nodded, looking defeated.

"Take back the power. You don't have to fight her, just quietly let her go. Then find new friends, real friends who actually care about you."

The girl's lip trembled. "All she has to do is say the word, and no one will have anything to do with me."

"That's not true. If you stand up to her, others will, too. Believe me, I've been there." Except, she also had Luke taking up for her, as well. "Think back to your old friends. I'm sure you'll find someone worth spending time with."

A light sparked in the girl's eyes. "I do have an

old friend." She groaned. "Oh, man. I've ignored her since hanging out with—"

"Mean Girl?"

She giggled.

"That's what I've dubbed her. Mean Girl. And she's not worth your time and energy. Move on. And, by the way, the pink pearls looked beautiful on you."

The girl's eyes watered, but a tremulous smile formed, then strengthened. "I'll take the necklace and the mom purse."

Darcy clapped her hands, overjoyed that this beautiful young woman was about to get out from under the peer pressure. "Oh, you just wait. My sister owns Chloe's Closet, and she assures me these bags are going to be huge this fall. Mean Girl won't be able to find one anywhere in town by then."

As they headed to the cash register, the girl tapped Darcy on the arm. "Thank you."

"No problem. Like I said, I've been in your shoes before. In fact, that man who left a few minutes ago is my oldest friend, the one who stood by me through the teasing and meanness."

"Wow, I wish I had a gorgeous friend like that." She laughed as she pulled out her debit card. "Of course, I'd probably fall in love with him and make a mess of it. But it would be nice to have him on my side for a while."

For a while.

Was Luke only for a while? Was their past together going to be enough to keep the friendship going, especially in this dangerous new territory they'd been navigating?

"Nothing ventured, nothing gained," Darcy said as she sat down next to Luke on the O'Malleys' patio glider after her shift at the mall, preparing to call Bryan.

Luke had driven her home after work, and she'd invited him to hang around and wait for news on a possible donation. Settling beside her, he put his arm along the back of the two seater so his shoulders wouldn't crowd her.

She was so beautiful in the moonlight, her creamy, freckled skin so smooth. How had he never noticed before this visit home? Had their close friendship blinded him to the fact she was a gorgeous, smart, giving woman?

She was his best friend first and always. He had to remember that.

"Here goes..." Darcy touched the call button on Bryan's old cell phone number in her contacts.

A pang of irritation shot through him once again. The fact that there was something about Darcy he didn't know, a relationship she'd never mentioned, outright bugged him.

He thought they'd told each other everything.

They sat close enough that he heard the phone ring twice.

"Darcy, it's great to hear from you!" a deep, resonant voice said, loud enough that it sounded as if they were on speakerphone.

Yes, Luke was eavesdropping but, since he was part of the fund-raiser, he didn't move away.

"Hey, Bryan. How's it going?" Darcy said, glancing at Luke.

Luke smiled and gave a nod of approval.

"Everything is going great. How about you? You're all done with school now, aren't you?"

"Yes, and thanks again for the graduation gift. I loved the CD."

Luke sneered. He'd sent a CD?

"Glad you liked it. So what are you doing now?"

"I've been working at the hospital here in town."

"Congrats! So you're back in Appleton, huh?"

"Of course. Can't imagine being anywhere else."

"Married yet?"

Luke's heart cranked into high gear.

For some reason, Darcy's eyes zoomed to Luke's face. "Nope. Still single." She leaned away ever so slightly.

There wasn't any room to scoot. She was stuck, glued to his side, so he could hear the whole conversation.

"Are you still based in Atlanta?" Darcy asked.

"Yes, but I'm moving to Nashville in a few months. Maybe we can get together before then."

She placed her free hand against her cheek as if cooling it, as if embarrassed. He'd seen her do it a thousand times before.

"I'd love to see you," she said. "Though, I'm calling for a somewhat selfish reason."

"Anything for you, Darcy." Bryan's voice oozed confidence, oozed familiarity. And not one bit of nerdiness.

Eyes flashing to his, Darcy jumped in to explain about the Food4Kids program. While she told the drummer about the auction, and that they needed one big item to feature in their ad, Luke's insides cinched in a knot. *Anything for you, Darcy.* The tone of his voice…

This guy had a thing for Darcy. Could she develop one for him?

"I'd be glad to help any way I can," Bryan said.

"Oh, thank you! I can't believe I never thought to contact you in the first place." Her excitement kicked her voice up a notch into a girly, flirty pitch he'd never before associated with his best friend.

"No biggie," Bryan said.

"So would you like to donate tickets to a concert or a signed item of some sort? Whatever you'd be comfortable with."

Darcy grinned at Luke. Stewing inside, Luke gave her a thumbs-up.

"I doubt I can get the band together to come up there on such short notice, but I'd love to be there for the event if I won't be in the way. I can bring some signed items and VIP tickets."

"I wasn't expecting you to make the trip. I can drive down to pick up your donation."

How would she manage that? She barely had time to breathe.

Bryan chuckled in a deep, way-too-familiar way. "Darcy, you're the one person in our school who was consistently nice to me. I want to come… to see you."

Darcy sucked in a breath.

Luke battled the urge to grab her phone and sling it across the yard.

"Well, uh, it's been ages." Her hand went to her cheek again. "I'd enjoy seeing you, too. I look forward to it."

After a brief discussion of details, Darcy and Bryan agreed he would plan to spend the whole weekend of the event in Appleton.

Oh, joy.

She ended the call and stuck the phone in her pocket. "Wow. He's coming to the auction."

Luke forced his clenched teeth apart. "Yeah, I heard everything he said."

"Oh." Hand to cheek again. "You don't look happy. Do you think it'll cause too much commotion to have him here?"

Ridiculous. He should be pleased for the donation. "Do you expect a problem?"

"I don't think so, since people around here know him. He's going to email me a list of items he'll donate. So for now, let's say 'Concert tickets and personally autographed Bryan Winningham items' in our ad."

"Whatever you think is best."

She huffed. "Are you mad?"

"No, I'm glad we have the donation. Do you really think he's a big enough draw?"

"Well, he can't bring the rest of the members of his band but—"

"What's his band's name?"

When she told him, he let out a whistle. "I've heard of them. I had no idea that was *this* Bryan." Having items from the up and coming band could be really good for his mom's ministry—if he could get over himself and his insane irritation at Bryan. "Nice work, Darcy. Glad you befriended him in high school."

"Are you saying I'm using him?" she said.

"Sorry. Didn't mean it that way. I'm actually relieved. Should be a good auction."

She leaned back and looked up at the stars, letting out a sigh. "Yeah. I think we could definitely meet our goal."

The tension flowed out of him. Honestly, he needed to get a grip.

Darcy had a friend years ago. The guy was interested in her. So what? This drummer could actually be The One for her. Luke had to be prepared for that. Maybe the timing of this was part of God's plans for Darcy.

The light from the moon played on her shiny hair as she angled her head to better see the night sky, placing her head nearly on his shoulder. "Look how beautiful. A waning gibbous moon."

"A what?"

"I've told you about it before."

As she once again explained about moon phases, all he could concentrate on was how close she was, how good she smelled—like flowers and everything sweet, sweet like her.

How could he ever separate the Darcy he grew up with and depended on from this woman who attracted him like crazy?

He couldn't. That was the problem. If he allowed the attraction to lead to its logical conclusion, he'd end up hurting her and lose his lifelong friend, his support, the person he'd always depended on for honesty. The person who would always be there for him if he needed anything.

She lifted her head off his shoulder and looked into his eyes. "You're not listening, are you?"

Focus. He had to ignore thoughts of her shiny hair and the smell of her perfume. Thoughts of her sparkling eyes and full lips. He had to concentrate on the geeky girl, the friend who'd tutored him through math and science.

"Tell me more about this gibbs thing," he said.

"Gibbous, Luke." She laughed and leaned close. "You goof."

"But you love this goof."

She shoved him in the shoulder. "You wish."

Yes. Unfortunately, at the moment, he did wish.

Chapter Seven

Luke's dad left for his office early Saturday morning as usual. Luke picked up breakfast and two cups of coffee at the café and carried it to the other side of the downtown square, one block from Rome Street.

If he was successful, he would kill two birds with one stone this morning. Persuade his dad to move to join his law practice, which might also serve to speed the end of the ill-advised relationship between Burt and Noreen.

The old Victorian home that housed Burt's office had been renovated a decade earlier and stood tall and proud, flanked by two giant magnolia trees that nearly touched the ground. The sign out front read Burt Jordan, Attorney at Law. At one time, Luke had imagined that sign would someday read Jordan & Jordan.

The familiar smell of paper and books and furniture polish brought back memories of working there in summers during high school. “I always loved this place.”

“You used to beg to come to work with me when you were little.” The smile his dad gave him eased some of the tension of the past few days. Being in this building did the same.

Burt nodded down the hallway toward his personal office and conference room. “Thanks for bringing breakfast. Let’s eat while it’s hot.”

Luke glanced at the receptionist’s desk, though Inez was much more than a receptionist. She’d been Dad’s assistant for twenty years. “How’s Inez doing these days?”

“Doing well. She’s on vacation this week, kicking up her heels in Daytona Beach.” His dad stopped at the last door on the right. “In here or the conference room?”

“Here’s fine.”

Inside his dad’s office, a massive wood desk sat in front of a wall of windows. Outside, a huge live oak stood sentinel over the backyard that was bordered by pines. Bluish-purple hydrangeas below the window added a touch of color to the scenery.

Burt settled at his desk while Luke pulled a sausage biscuit out of the bag and handed over a steaming cup. Once Luke had his own food, he sat in the leather chair on the other side of the desk.

With fingers steepled under his chin, Burt

locked his gaze on his son. "So why the meeting this morning?"

"Wanted to touch base since we've been going in different directions lately." *And since you've been avoiding me.* Luke took his time adding cream to his coffee and stirring, uncertain how he should approach the topic of asking his dad to move to Nashville. "The painters and roofers did a good job this past week. House is looking good."

"Yes, a new coat did a lot to brighten up the exterior."

"Other than occasionally supervising workers, I feel like I haven't been much help at home. However, I have a nice ceremony planned that will honor Mom at the Food4Kids auction. I'm going to ask Granny to speak, to tell how Mom came up with the idea of the program and give a report on the number of kids served since its inception."

While sipping from the rim of his cup, his dad's eyes shone gratitude. "Your mom would've been happy to know you're involved."

"I also asked the mayor to speak, to honor Mom. I'd like it if you could come."

"Of course. Wouldn't miss it."

They ate in silence for several minutes. Luke hesitated to tackle the main topic he'd come to discuss. He took a deep breath, ready to toss the idea out there.

"I appreciate the ceremony for your mom. It's

exactly what I'd been hoping for." Burt set down his coffee cup with finality. "But I'm not selling the house."

Luke slowly placed his coffee on the desk. Though he hated the thought of letting the house go, this wasn't the news he'd wanted to hear. "I see."

His dad had never been good at communicating. At least not feelings. After a few moments of silence, Luke figured that he wouldn't get any further explanation.

Leaning back with elbows propped on the arms of the chair, clasped palms folded under his chin, Burt watched Luke.

"You seem disappointed," Burt said. He was sharp. Didn't miss a thing, which was what made him a good attorney.

The refusal to sell was a definite wrinkle in Luke's plan. He could understand Burt's attachment to the house, yet he suspected this had more to do with Noreen—who could end up being a much bigger wrinkle than a house. "I want you to do what's best for you."

Burt nodded. "I am as happy as I can be, considering what we've been through. I truly care for Noreen and feel hopeful for the first time in a long time."

"I'm afraid you're rushing into something you're

not ready for yet. Don't you think maybe you're depending on her too much?"

"No, I don't." Burt wadded up the biscuit wrapper and shoved it into the brown paper bag. "Your mom made me promise to move on and live my life after she was gone. I think—" He cleared his throat and looked away. "I'm trying to honor her wishes."

Luke had heard his mom make that request of his dad. Still, romance was blinding the man. He couldn't see potential problems.

"Dad, I'd like—"

Burt threw his hand up to stop him. "I expect you to honor your mother's wishes as well, by supporting me on this."

What could Luke do in light of that request? Would his mom really want his dad to move on so quickly? Luke didn't think so, and it frustrated him to no end that Burt wouldn't at least slow down, take his time before diving headfirst into dating.

No matter, his dad wouldn't be budging on the issue today. "I'll try." He took one last sip of his coffee and then gathered their trash. "I'll let you get back to work. I've got to check in with Roger, then Darcy and I are going to the lake to open the house."

Burt's shoulders relaxed, his eyes lit with pleasure. "Take a picnic. Plan to roast marshmallows and enjoy yourselves."

"We'll be working, but we'll try to have fun."

"Oh, I don't think you have to try too hard with Darcy. You two know each other so well it's like you're two halves of a whole."

The thought made breathing difficult, which happened a lot around Darcy lately. Stress must be getting to him.

For now, though, he'd focus on getting through one day.

Darcy finished dusting, sweeping and mopping the lake house. Though someone had to have already been to the house that spring. She'd hardly found a speck of dust or dirt.

Now that the kitchen was stocked with nonperishables, the auction winners would be able to come any week they'd like.

Time to find out how Luke was progressing on the boat.

Darcy wove her way through a small cluster of trees along the path that led to the dock. As she approached, she slowed, peeking through branches to find Luke inspecting the life preservers.

She'd always loved watching him on the boat. He was at home and totally relaxed, as if he'd been created to be on the water. He'd been as good on water skis as at anything else he attempted, a natural athlete.

Continuing down the path, she walked out of the woods into the open.

"Oh, hey. Done cleaning the house already?" Luke asked. "I was going to come up and help you finish."

"All done. And either our parents are senile, or else they didn't tell the whole truth about coming up here this season."

"I agree. The dock and boat were in great shape."

"I suspect my mom wanted to make sure I took a day off."

He didn't respond, simply stood on the boat, hands on his hips, with a grin big enough to rival the sunshine.

"Luke Jordan, did you have something to do with this?"

"Nope." He laid a hand to his chest. "Cross my heart. But I think you're right."

He hopped off the boat onto the dock, the weathered wood swaying with his heavy footsteps. When he reached the covered area set up with lawn chairs and picnic table, he grabbed a canvas bag and handed it to her. "Your mom sent this."

Inside, Darcy found her swimsuit, a beach towel and bottle of sunscreen. "Yep. She knew we'd end up with free time."

"I brought my trunks just in case. How about taking the boat out for a swim?"

She *was* hot from cleaning. And she did have a free afternoon. "Sure. Why not?"

They headed back to the house to change, planning to meet up again at the boat.

When Darcy arrived, she found Luke in the driver's seat, ready to go, with sunglasses on and the key in the ignition. "About time."

"Mr. Impatient." She stowed her belongings and went to the cushioned seating at the front of the ski boat, eager for the rush of speed on the water.

Luke started the engine and backed away from the dock. Then he pushed the throttle forward, slowly moving out of the cove. Once they reached open water, he opened up the engine, sending them speeding across the lake.

Wind whipped her hair, and a fine mist of water cooled her as the boat bumped over the wake created by a nearby boat. She closed her eyes, her face directly in the breeze, and enjoyed the thrill of freedom. She'd always adored being out on the lake, just the two of them with the wind, sun and water.

Soon, Luke pulled into their favorite cove and killed the engine. The isolated spot was small and perfect for swimming.

"No pushing me," she called. "The water is probably freezing cold. I need to ease in."

Slowly taking off his sunglasses, a predatory gleam lit his eyes. "You know how I feel about easing into the water."

She squealed and laughed as he walked near. "I'm serious! No throwing me overboard."

Right before he got to her, he changed direction, yanked off his T-shirt and jumped over the side of the boat making a big splash. "Come on. The water is perfect."

She peeked over the edge of the boat and watched as he swam around. "You're just saying that."

"I'll give you two minutes to do this the slow way. After that...well, I won't be held responsible for my actions."

From past experience, she knew he meant business. He didn't tolerate wimps.

With a huge smile on her face, and memories of all the times they'd had similar conversations warming her inside, she removed her cover-up and went to the back of the boat. Sitting on the edge of the swim platform, she splashed water on her legs and slowly inched her way in up to her shoulders, the cool water taking her breath away momentarily.

"This water is *not* perfect," she called. "Maybe it will be by July when it's burning hot outside." Looking around, she couldn't find Luke. Which usually made her nervous.

Suddenly, he burst through the water not a foot from her. "About time you got wet."

"Hey, you know I like to do things differently," she said, treading water. "You yank off bandages, and I like to slowly pull them off."

"It's less painful to just dive in."

His brown eyes sparkled as his strong arms wove back and forth, treading water to keep him nearby.

If only she was the type to do that. To risk all. To go for everything she wanted in life without thinking.

As he swam closer, she took hold of the swim platform. He grabbed hold beside her, his hand touching hers.

"I'm glad we have today," Luke said, slicking back his wet hair. Water ran off his tanned, muscular arm resting beside hers. Familiar brown eyes locked with hers, and he smiled.

How was it possible for his smile to make her chest ache?

She swallowed, his nearness making it difficult to speak. "Me, uh—" She cleared her throat. "I'm glad, too."

The sun made his eyes lighter than usual, the gold flecks sparkling and bright. He looked happy. Relaxed. More relaxed than he'd looked since he arrived.

"Being in your old stomping grounds is good for you," she said. "You seem content."

The water swirled between them, and she floated closer. Too close. She'd float right into his arms if she wasn't careful.

"On the lake, I can pretend I'm on vacation."

"Yeah, me, too. A much-needed vacation."

Luke glanced up at her hair, a flash of mischief entering his eyes. "You still haven't gotten all the way in. I think it's been way more than two minutes."

"Don't you dare." She squealed as she darted away.

He took slow, deliberate strokes to catch up, intent on catching her. She kicked her feet launching herself away from him even as she splashed water at his face. Laughing so hard she thought she might inhale half the lake, she took off toward the boat. She grabbed the back of the boat and gasped for breath, still laughing.

Once again, Luke was hidden somewhere underwater.

"I'm a goner."

At the same moment Luke's head broke through the water, his hand shot up and dunked her under.

She came back up, sputtering and coughing, water dripping in her eyes and was met with his gloating grin, an expression of utter satisfaction.

She laughed as she wiped her eyes. "I'm glad I can make you so happy."

"Yanked off that bandage," he called with a grin as he swam away to take a few laps around the boat.

She held her ribs that ached from laughing.

Luke Jordan would never change. She didn't want him to.

Smiling, she climbed back in the boat, dried off and put on her cover-up. She stretched out her legs along the seat in the front, soaking up the warm rays of the sun.

Before long, Luke joined her, lounging on the seat across from her with knees bent since his legs were too long for the space. The sway of the water lulled them.

How many times had they done this on a lazy summer day?

"Do you remember that fall break when I tossed you in the water wearing your new sweater?" he said, pulling her out of her stupor.

"How could I forget? I nearly drowned from the weight of that oversize thick cotton knit."

He chuckled, deep and rich, the sound sending chills along her arms.

"Hey, I jumped in to rescue you. In my jeans. With my wallet."

She'd been secretly thrilled, even while furious with him. "That sweater stretched so badly it never did fit the same."

He tilted his head and looked over at her. "And my cheek never recovered. If I remember, you smacked me pretty hard."

"No, the smack was from when you treated my first love so badly he ended up dumping me."

"Oh, yeah." He snorted. "That guy in graduate school. You didn't love that loser."

She thought she had. For a few minutes, anyway. "You were so rude to Randy. Hardly gave him the time of day."

"He wasn't worthy of you."

"He was a good guy with a bright future in microbiology."

Luke laughed. "You two made perfect study partners. Didn't mean you should marry him."

Turned out, Luke was right. She and Randy had enjoyed each other's company, but she'd never felt the sort of attraction she'd hoped for. The type of spark she'd felt lately.

Unable to deny Luke's claim, she huffed.

"See, I know you well enough to know who'll make you happy."

She sat up and faced him. "Okay, Mr. Know It All. Just who *will* make me happy?"

On the other side of the boat, forearms resting on his thighs, he looked into her eyes. A few feet separated them, but she felt as if they were a mere breath apart as his gaze drilled into hers, sucking the air out of her lungs, making her face burn like the hot Georgia sun.

For as long as he could remember, Luke thought he'd known what was best for Darcy. Now he began to wonder. Could he be objective? "I think we'll both know when you've found the right one."

Looking away, Darcy ran her fingers through her hair, slicking the strands away from her face. "Ha! So are you going to give me final approval when *you* fall in love?"

"I already did that with Raquel. You gave your vote by backing away from me." Which, at the time had left him confused, alone, hurting.

"Hey, I gave you room for what's her name when you said you were in love."

He couldn't help but grin. Darcy never did want to say Raquel's name and showed utter disgust every time she mentioned her. Whether she would admit it or not, Darcy, too, had gone into protect mode. She'd warned that Raquel would hurt him.

He'd actually dodged a big mistake. The worst part had been the fallout with Darcy.

"I still don't get why *what's her name* bothered you so much." He grinned at using the nickname.

Darcy glanced away. "You really don't get it, do you? Every time a girl would start to get serious or mention the word *love,* you'd freak and break up. But *what's her name,*" she said with an arched brow and teasing smile, "was different. You broke the friend code. You brought Raquel into our relationship—on the picnic, inviting her to study with us, asking me to bring her home for the weekend. You obviously loved her, and for the first time ever, you didn't need me." She kept her tone light and playful, but he could see hurt in her eyes.

He crossed the boat to sit beside her, pushed her hair over her shoulder. "Seems like there may have been something deeper going on than simply breaking the friend code with Raquel."

With a quiet laugh, she shook her head. "What if I told you I had a terrible crush on you?"

Her admission slammed into him, stealing away his breath. "A crush? On *me?*"

"Yep." Looking relieved and terrified at the same time, Darcy scrunched up her nose and nodded. She cautiously watched him, as if observing every nuance of his reaction.

So many things in their past now made sense.

"Wow." He shook his head. "Ironic, then, that what I thought was love for Raquel didn't last past the first argument, which was over the fact that Raquel thought I loved you."

She looked into his eyes. "Crazy, huh?"

"I wish you would have told me."

She laughed and lifted her face to the sun, eyes

closed. "Oh, yeah, that would have gone over really well. You would have tossed my broken heart aside along with all the others, and I would have lost my best friend."

Based on his history, she was probably right. "I'm sorry if I hurt you."

She reached for the bottle of sunscreen and flipped open the top. "I got over it. We were friends again before long."

Yeah, they were, but it bothered him to know she'd hidden her feelings from him. Bothered him that she would hide anything from him.

"Come on. Let's go back to the house." He put on his sunglasses and went to the captain's chair.

"Nothing like a little spilled guts to kill the fun of a day on the lake, huh?" She tilted her head and smiled at him letting him know she was okay.

"Yeah, this heart-to-heart has worn me out." He laughed as the boat burst to life then guided them back to their little cove on the other side of the lake.

Once they pulled up to the dock, and he cut the engine, Darcy got up to gather her belongings. "I guess we're even now."

"How so?"

"You ran off Randy, and I ran off Raquel."

"Sort of." Luke had hurt Darcy, wanted her to better understand his breakup. "Only, Raquel didn't break up with me."

Darcy's eyes widened, surprised with his admission. "She didn't?"

"Once I realized I'd somehow messed up with you, I knew Raquel didn't matter to me as much as you did. That was a big aha moment."

"A tribute to our lifelong friendship." She put a warm, soft hand on his arm. "Thank goodness we got back to normal."

Normal? He hadn't felt normal around her since he'd returned home and been blown away by this strange attraction. When he looked into her deep blue eyes now, something flared to life. He could almost imagine she felt something was different, too.

She reached around and grabbed her towel and bag. "I guess we're done up here at the lake house. Time to go back to town."

He tethered the boat, hopped out onto the dock and held out his hand to help her off the boat.

Darcy glanced from his hand to his face with a big smile. "No tricks? I don't want to go back in that freezing water."

"That water's at least seventy degrees."

"And my body is ninety-eight point six," she said with a laugh.

He smiled at the priceless expression on her face. She was torn between fear of a frequent prank and trusting him. "No tricks," he said.

As she reached for his hand, she stared into his

eyes, watching for indications of his intent. At the last second, she snatched her arm back to her side. "Promise?"

With a laugh, he lunged for her, picked her up by the waist and then set her safely on the dock, leaving his hands in place. "Trust me now?"

"Not when it comes to lake water." She chuckled. "But there's still hope. You'll have to prove yourself over time."

She pulled away and tossed her tote bag over her shoulder. "I'm going to go shower and dress."

"Meet me back at the fire pit. I have a surprise for you."

He watched as she headed toward the path to the house, a friend who was so much more. And who had no idea how much he was beginning to care.

Darcy looked in the dresser mirror in the tiny upstairs bedroom she and Chloe still shared while at the lake as she thought of what Luke had said.

He'd broken up with Raquel. Not the other way around.

Wow. If she'd only known that back then…

Then what? She would have told him how she felt? No way.

Besides, she didn't need to let her mind wander in those crazy directions.

Glancing around the room, she smiled at how much she loved this place. The furniture was sparse and utilitarian, pieces Noreen and Joan had picked up at yard sales through the years. They'd furnished the house on a shoestring budget, especially since the kids spent all their waking hours outdoors.

Today, Darcy had enjoyed taking her time getting ready in the peaceful setting, time she couldn't take on a normal workday. Today had been the perfect, relaxing getaway she'd needed.

She ran a brush through her hair and packed up her wet swimsuit and towel. Normally, she would hang her wet items and leave them for the next weekend trip. Since she and Luke were preparing for the auction winner, she tidied the room, tossed her bag in the car, then headed to the fire pit.

A small campfire crackled and popped as the logs shifted and settled. Sunlight, filtering through the tall pines, dappled Luke's damp hair with light and shadows. When he spotted her, he smiled, totally relaxed and at home in another of the places they'd spent so much of their childhood and teen years.

"I still feel a little guilty," she said. "Like we should be working, not playing."

A bag of hot dogs and package of buns sat on top of a cooler next to Luke.

"What's this?"

"A late lunch."

Nearby, she discovered graham crackers, marshmallows and chocolate bars. "Oh, and the makings for s'mores? What a nice surprise."

He looked away. "Dad suggested it." He spread the wood with a heavy stick to lower the flames and expose some embers.

Darcy sat on one of the logs that circled the area, skewered two long, thin sticks lengthwise with hot dogs, and then handed one to Luke.

He plopped down beside her and held the meat over the red-hot embers. As his hair dried, the slicked-back sections morphed into his regular unmanageable waves, falling across his brow.

"We've had some good times here," he said, staring into the flames.

"We have." Not counting the summer he'd gone head-over-heels over Chloe and had barely noticed Darcy was alive.

"This is my favorite place on earth." He looked into her eyes, gently bumped her shoulder with his. "Only when you're around, of course."

"Of course." She laughed and stared into the fire, her stomach a jumble of nerves for some reason.

When her hot dog started to blacken and bubble on one side, she turned it. Luke's was doing the same, only he wasn't actually paying attention. She reached out, took hold of his hand and turned it. "You're burning."

"You've always kept me on track."

She grinned as she thought of the many times she'd forced him to study or helped him on projects. "It's a dirty job, but someone's gotta do it."

"Hey, be kind. I took up for you every now and then." With a chuckle, he reached for a bun, nestled the hot dog inside, then slid out the roasting stick and set his food on a plate. Then he started the whole process over again with another one.

Her heart squeezed as she recalled the times when someone at school had made fun of her for being such a bookworm, and Luke had charged in to defend her. All it took was one word from big strong Luke Jordan to send them packing.

She leaned into one of those big strong shoulders, breathing in the scent of fresh shampoo with a touch of smoke. "By the way, I took your advice and urged that girl at Glenda's to stand up to Mean Girl."

"I'm glad." He nodded as if approving.

She slipped her hot dog into a bun but set it on a plate. Yeah, she used to think of Luke as her knight in shining armor. Always present. Always looking out for her.

"You know, since your mom said you have no social life, maybe I've assumed too much," he said. "Is there anyone I need to protect you from these days? Anyone been breaking your heart?"

No one but you, she wanted to say. She looked into his eyes and was transported right back to the old familiar ache, longing to push that now-dry hair off his forehead, longing to tell him she cared about him as much more than a friend. Only those longings weren't merely a distant memory.

She had allowed herself to fall for him all over again. Would she never be able to get over Luke? If she couldn't have him, would she never manage to have a future with any other man?

"Sorry," she said. "No dragons for you to slay. There's no man in my life right now."

"No?" He slowly turned the stick, roasting another hot dog.

She sighed. Might as well tell him the thoughts she'd been having. "I suspect God intends for me to remain single."

"Now why would you think something like that?"

"I don't know. I've had a feeling, like I need to quit dreaming of Prince Charming sweeping me off my feet and learn to be content with my life."

"Maybe God is leading you to be content right before he's going to bring some amazing guy into your life. Could even be Bryan."

She looked over at Luke, his profile strong and serious as he focused his attention on putting the second hot dog in a bun. No smile lines. No teasing.

"I doubt that," she said. "Which is why I'm eager to pay off my loans now that Mom is dating. I need to be prepared to move out quickly, need to be financially independent."

"What you *need* to do is quit that extra job so you have time to live your life. Time to meet someone nice who deserves you." The sadness in his eyes touched her deeply. He couldn't mean those words, not the way he was looking at her.

Without hesitation, she reached out and, like a dozen girls before her, pushed the wayward hair back from his brow. She was as big a sucker as the rest of them. But if this would be her only chance, why not take it?

Surprise flashed in his eyes, and she felt the recent sense of awareness sizzle between them. Yet he didn't move away or even comment.

"I imagine you'll settle in Nashville," she said, "meet Miss Right, get married and have two-point-five kids and a minivan." She sighed and leaned her head against his shoulder. "I wonder how it'll affect our friendship, once there's a Mrs. Luke Jordan?"

He laid his cheek against the top of her head. "I can't imagine that. I've never been able to see anyone in that role."

"Even with the many women you've dated?"

"Not one."

She pulled away from him, tempted by his strong shoulder, not wanting to get too cozy.

"Aren't we a pair? Neither of us sees a future with marriage and happily ever after."

Brushing her hair over her shoulder, he ran his fingers through the long strands, raising chill bumps along her arm.

"You're a great catch, Darcy. Some guy will be lucky to get you." His gaze dipped to her lips, and she realized this was no food-on-her-chin alert. This was the real thing.

He hesitated, as if he expected her to laugh in his face or pull away. She simply swallowed past the big knot of fear, and yes, joy, clogging her throat. When she didn't flee, his hand cupped the back of her head and drew her closer.

Right before their lips touched, he looked into her eyes with a flash of uncertainty.

She didn't move. Just held her breath.

Warm, full lips touched hers, tentatively at first. Soft lips she'd merely dreamed about. She placed her hand on his chest, felt the wild beat of his heart.

He pulled her closer, and like a match to tinder, deepened the kiss, plunging his hands into her hair.

Closer, she wanted to be closer. She wrapped her arms around his neck and held on tightly, joyous.

He groaned, pulled away slightly and rested his forehead against hers. "Darcy," he whispered, his voice full of the longing she felt. Then he cupped her face in his hands and tilted his head, bringing her lips to his once again.

This was what she'd been waiting for since the age of fifteen. She poured a decade of longing into a kiss so perfect that she never wanted it to end.

Without warning, he jerked away, gasping for breath. He stood, jamming both hands into his hair, pushing it back from his face. "What in the world have we done?"

She remained rooted to the log, her heart breaking into tiny jagged pieces she knew she'd be unable to put back together.

"That was a huge mistake." He picked up their plates and shoved them into a trash bag. "I mean, we have a friendship to protect. And goals that take us in different directions. We can't let ourselves be sidetracked."

She nodded, unable to speak. What could she say after he'd called their kiss a huge mistake? Tell him that had been the best moment of her life?

How pathetic. Don't sit here like a bump on a log. The irony of the thought nearly forced out a hysterical laugh, yet tears stung her nose.

She would. Not. Cry.

Luke lifted the lid to the cooler and dumped everything inside—chocolate bars, graham crackers and a bag of marshmallows.

Anger and humiliation drove her to her feet.

He looked at her, finally, his expression pleading with her to understand. "We can't make the same mistake our parents are making."

Obviously, a kiss had nearly ruined everything with Luke. She couldn't imagine a future without his friendship. "Remember Chloe," she said through an aching throat.

With his hands stuffed in his pockets, he stood there and nodded. "Yeah. That's right. Like I told Dad, you can't let romance mess up a friendship. Especially not one that only comes along once in a lifetime."

Without another word, they locked up the house and loaded the car, then drove back to Appleton in silence. As the scenery whizzed by, thoughts of their first and only kiss flashed through Darcy's mind.

How could a kiss that wonderful be wrong?

Of course, he was right. Yet it didn't make it any easier to let go of a longtime dream.

Chapter Eight

When Luke pulled into his driveway, he didn't know how he'd managed to drive home. The whole trip was a blur. Between reliving the kiss and watching Darcy in his peripheral vision, he'd barely concentrated on the road.

He put the car in Park and cut the engine. He had to acknowledge her. Had to act as normal as possible. She was the only person besides his mother and grandmother he'd ever been able to depend on, who would stick by his side no matter what, success or failure.

Darcy was off-limits. Was too deserving and sweet for someone like him who'd never before committed to long-term.

How could he have risked blowing their friendship for a kiss? Granted, a life changing, mind-shattering kiss. But a kiss, nonetheless.

He turned to her, forcing himself to make eye

contact. "We're here. Thanks for helping get the house ready."

She smiled, but the devastation in her eyes nearly broke his heart. She probably couldn't stand the thought that she was attracted to him of all people. She saw him as superficial when it came to dating relationships. Had always chided him, acted disapproving when he broke up with girlfriend after girlfriend. She'd be mortified to think she could be lumped in with that list of women.

"Anything for the kids." Her hand fluttered to the door handle. "Well, gotta go."

He needed to stay away from her to make sure he didn't do anything stupid, but he couldn't be rude. "I'll walk you home."

She held up her hand to stop him. "No, thanks. I'm good."

As she climbed out of the passenger side, he exited the car. Then he watched as she hurried home.

What have we done?

Had they ruined everything? Surely not. They'd spoken civilly, agreed that the kiss had been a mistake. And they still needed to cooperate with each other on the auction.

Everything would turn out fine, as long as he pushed the day's events out of his mind and resolved not to give in to the temptation to kiss her again.

Now that he'd seen the slippery slope of giving in to attraction, he knew he needed to warn his dad about doing the same thing with Noreen.

Luke went inside and found his dad in his home office, sitting at the desk, still in his shirt and tie with the tie loosened.

"I'm glad I caught you at home," Luke said.

"Productive day?"

Depended on the definition of *productive.* He had certainly produced a disaster. "Yeah, the house was in good shape. Someone must've already been up there this season."

A guilty flush colored Burt's cheeks. "Uh, yeah. Maybe so."

Had their parents played matchmaker, then? "Look, Dad. I need to talk to you. And it's not easy."

He shut his laptop. "Have a seat."

"I've probably been a little too outspoken with my opinion of you and Noreen dating. Now I've had time to calm down some and see you together."

Burt nodded. "I knew you'd come around."

"I still feel I need to warn you about moving too quickly. Mom's only been gone six months. We're still grieving."

"Six months *is* a short time. But I was here with your mom all along, had more time to prepare for losing her. Noreen has been a widow for over two years and has helped me work through my grief. I've had help healing that you haven't had."

"Dad, I'm worried about Noreen, too. I see how attached she is to you. What if this attraction you've had for her is simply out of grief and loneliness?"

"It's not."

"What if, down the road, you find it is? She'll be crushed."

Burt's brows drew together. Was Luke finally getting through to him?

"I don't take your concerns lightly," Burt said. "I promise you I'll be careful."

Encouraged, Luke scooted to the edge of his seat, leaning forward, forearms on knees. "Dad, I know you don't want to sell the house, but I'd like to propose something I've considered for several weeks. I think the arrangement could be good for both of us."

"I'm always open to your ideas."

As long as Luke could remember, he'd wanted to make his dad proud. Asking him for help would be difficult. Yet he'd never know his dad's reaction if he didn't try.

"The Nashville practice is thriving, growing faster than either Roger or I dreamed."

Burt crossed his arms and smiled. "That's great news."

"Roger will be fully retired in the next few

months, and he's ready to turn the practice over to me. Frankly, I'm concerned clients may feel I don't have enough experience."

"You'll learn. I think you can do it."

The vote of confidence settled inside him, balm for that place of doubt he'd carried for too long. "I appreciate that. But a couple of clients have already left, citing my lack of experience. I need someone I can trust, someone with your experience. I'd like for you to join me as my partner."

His dad plunked back in his chair, brows raised. "I didn't see that coming."

"I like to think you'd be happy up there. New challenges, new setting."

"Son, I don't mean to be flippant, but I can't envision that partnership working."

The words pained him, yet wasn't that what he'd expected from his father? "I hope you can set aside your feelings for Noreen to at least consider the offer. If nothing else, you and I would live closer to each other."

"This has nothing to do with Noreen. I wouldn't want to move and begin again when I'm starting to think of retirement myself. Besides, I think you'd be happier if you settled here in your hometown with Darcy."

It was Luke's turn to plunk back in his chair, blown away by his dad's keen perception. Or, rather, *mis*perception.

Who was Luke kidding? His dad wasn't off base. Were his feelings for Darcy that obvious?

"I'm committed to Roger, to the practice," Luke said.

"I'm proud of you for that. But no one would fault you for leaving an associate position to return to your hometown. Better now than after Roger retires."

What did Burt think Luke would do? Move home and open a solo practice down the road? Join another local firm?

"I closed on the building last week. I'm staying in Nashville."

"If that's your decision, then maybe it's time to talk with other attorneys in the area about joining you."

If his dad wouldn't consider the offer, then Luke was wasting his time. He needed to get out of Appleton as soon as possible. To keep his friendship with Darcy intact.

Darcy paced the length of the kitchen counter. Where was her mom?

She glanced at her cell phone for the hundredth time. Was Mom with Burt? She hadn't answered any of Darcy's texts since she'd gotten home from the lake.

Mrs. Johnson, Darcy's boss at the mall, had certainly answered, though. And she was not happy

Darcy had called in sick for the first time ever. The text she sent Darcy as follow-up left no doubt that the manager was disappointed in Darcy and not happy to have to stay late and close the store.

Darcy was in pain, though, physical and otherwise. Her stomach…her heart. There was no way she could go in and act cheerful around customers, no way she could focus to count a drawer full of money and total out a cash register.

All Luke's fault.

If she were honest, her own fault, as well. She'd known…*known*…not to let herself fall for him again.

"Darcy, honey, where are you?" Mom called from the foyer.

Finally. "In the kitchen."

Noreen rushed through the doorway. "Are you okay? I was helping Chloe mark down sale items and just now saw your texts."

"I'm fine." Or she would be.

With a hand pressed to her chest, Noreen sagged against the counter. "You sounded frantic to find me."

"I'm sorry. I didn't know where you were, and I need to talk to you."

Tossing her purse and keys on the counter, Noreen huffed out a breath of relief. "Then let's go outside and chat."

They sat side by side on the glider, and when

her mom pushed Darcy's hair over her shoulder like Luke had done, she wanted to cry.

"What's wrong, honey?"

"I'm worried about you," she blurted to keep from admitting she was worried about herself, as well. Determined to keep her mom from experiencing the same pain of rejection, she decided she had to plow ahead. "I know you're happy dating Burt. And I truly love to see that. But you have to promise me you'll avoid falling for him."

Noreen's face glowed with an expression of bliss so sweet and tender Darcy's eyes stung.

"I'm afraid it's too late for that. I love him. I just haven't told him yet."

"Mom, nooo."

"You've been so supportive. Why the sudden protectiveness?"

How could she explain that Burt was probably like his son, and that he'd freak when she said she loved him, and would push her away?

The same as Luke always did. Every girl who ever got close to him and dared mention love—or even seriously dating—sent him in the opposite direction. He had some kind of off switch that emotional closeness tripped, something that kept him from loving them back.

"You're a wonderful woman," Darcy said, "but I'm afraid Burt's simply lonely and will change his mind once he's had time to heal."

"A risk I'm willing to take. I respect him and truly feel he knows what he's doing. He understands our relationship has moved very quickly. But, honey, we both feel Joan and your dad would be happy for us."

Scared for her mom, yet touched by her sincerity, Darcy grabbed Noreen's hand and held tight.

"With their illnesses and deaths, Burt and I have learned a hard lesson about taking life and love for granted. We want to live fully now."

How could Darcy argue with that? "Please don't do anything crazy like get married, okay? Give him time to make sure you're The One."

"Are you sure your fear isn't colored by something else?"

Her eyes locked with her mom's. "What do you mean?"

"I sense there's more to your relationship with Luke than longtime friendship."

Darcy's heart pattered against her ribs. "Nope. We learned our lesson when he dated Chloe. In fact, today we mentioned our old mantra about that."

Noreen's expression turned sad. "You can deny it to me if you're not ready to talk, but you need to at least be honest with yourself."

Darcy glanced around the patio at the planters of freshly planted petunias, the neatly trimmed hedges, the comfy chaise longue. Finally her gaze landed back on her mother.

"I don't know what to do without ruining everything," Darcy whispered.

Noreen pulled her close for a hug. "Oh, honey, just follow your heart."

Follow her heart? After that devastating kiss and Luke's reaction to it? Her heart had led her astray every time before. Had led her to unrequited love and heartbreak.

No, Darcy needed to get her act together. Had to wrestle back her feelings for Luke and not let them show if she wanted to retain her dignity. Which probably meant an end to their easy friendship. She couldn't be relaxed around him without giving herself away.

Lord, is there something You're teaching me here? At the moment, I sure can't figure it out.

No one must know she was falling in love with Luke...especially Luke.

Chapter Nine

Out of the corner of his eye, Luke spotted Darcy, a mere blur of khaki and green zipping through the church doorway as soon as the Sunday morning service ended. She was avoiding him all together.

"Was that Darcy?" his grandmother asked, holding on to his arm.

"I think that was her."

"Hmm. Must be in a hurry."

Grace had that right. Apparently, Darcy wasn't up to acting as if nothing had happened yesterday. He couldn't say he blamed her. He wasn't sure he was ready, either.

Even though his conversation with Burt hadn't gone well the night before, Luke needed to tell Granny that he'd asked his dad to come to Tennessee. Needed to prepare her, in case Burt mentioned the offer.

"How about I take you out to lunch, Granny?"

"I believe your dad said he and Noreen had plans, so that sounds lovely."

They walked across the square to the café and got the last available table for two, a small half booth in the very back. The spot was typically used for waitresses to sit and wrap silverware, only used for customers during their busiest hours.

Once he and Granny had ordered, Luke heard the waitress showing a party to the booth behind him, the same one he and Chloe and Darcy had sat in the week before.

Though the voices were unfamiliar, one of the occupants spoke his mom's name.

Then his dad's name.

He glanced at Granny. Either she hadn't heard, or else she was trying to ignore the conversation, which wasn't flattering to either Noreen or Burt.

Luke clenched his teeth and took a deep breath, trying his best to hold his temper. "Granny, I'd like for you to speak at the auction. To tell how Food4Kids started, maybe tell some stats on how many kids have been helped."

Granny opened her mouth to reply, but the conversation behind them drew her attention.

"I can't believe Noreen would do that," said the woman in a pseudo-whisper. "I mean, come on. Her best friend's husband? So soon?"

Before he thought better of it, Luke slid out of

the booth and stepped to where he could see who was talking about Noreen and his dad.

He recognized one of the three women as the cashier of the local dollar store but didn't know her name. Her mouth fell open when she saw him.

"I couldn't help overhearing your conversation," Luke said in as friendly a tone as he could manage given the fury curling inside him. "Please refrain from speaking about Noreen that way. Gossip about this particular situation—which, by the way, is a private matter—is hurtful."

"I'm sorry," the stricken woman said. "No harm intended."

Yeah, right. He nodded and returned to his seat as she and her friends hustled out of the diner.

Granny patted his hand then motioned him closer. "Good job, son. Your dad would be proud to hear you taking up for Noreen." Her brown eyes reflected kindness, reassurance. "I'm glad to see you're changing your mind about their relationship."

"I haven't, Granny. In fact, last night I asked Dad to relocate to Nashville. I want to bring in a partner with experience, someone I can trust, and invited him to come join the practice."

He hated the concerned look on her face as she fiddled with the button at the neck of her blouse. "Did you really?"

"I'm sorry. I should have told you my plan as soon as I got to town. I'd like for you to come, too."

"What did Burt say?"

"What do you think?" He sighed and shook his head. "He's not going to leave Noreen unless something changes drastically. Which it could, once he comes to his senses."

She speared him with one of her censuring looks. "As much as I think you'd be happier moving back home, I should tell you I believe in you. You're perfectly capable of running that business on your own."

"Thanks, Granny. I've lost a couple of clients, but I'll be fine." He would have to be to make those mortgage payments.

Roger had said he'd be available to advise. Luke could find someone local who might like to join the firm. But Luke would have to give up on the chance to prove himself to his dad. It was time to be strong, to stand on his own. Time to prepare to leave Appleton as soon as the auction was over.

And maybe it was time, too, to move beyond the old friendship with Darcy. To let it go. Somehow, coming home and being around her never failed to stir up thoughts of settling back in Appleton, thoughts of settling *for* Appleton. It also stirred up thoughts of wanting to see Jordan & Jordan on that sign. Of wanting to be close by his grandmother. Of wanting to spend every free moment with Darcy.

And now, heaven help him, it stirred up thoughts of wanting to kiss her again.

Despite the detour his heart had taken lately, maybe it was time to sever that tie with Darcy. Time for both of them to move on to the lives God had planned for them.

Darcy managed to avoid Luke for three straight days. She knew she would eventually need to contact him about the auction, yet she planned to put it off as long as possible.

She'd just completed her second night in a row closing Glitzy Glenda's as penance for calling in sick on Saturday. Her feet ached. Her head pounded. Her stomach growled. Darcy was so tired she wanted to drop in her tracks and go to sleep on a bench in the middle of the mall.

She locked the gate, tossed the bag of trash into a large portable bin in the middle of the mall, then proceeded to the night deposit.

Soon, she'd be home.

Soon, she'd eat the warm vegetable soup her mom had promised to have waiting.

Soon, she'd— *Umpf,* she grunted as a hard shove from behind sent her flying toward the bank drop box even as her shoulder wrenched backward. Her hand smacked into the wall, but she caught herself before her head hit the teller machine. She gripped her neck and turned to see if she'd tripped or—

She hadn't tripped. Someone had pushed her. Someone who was now running out the door into the parking lot.

With her purse.

Stunned, Darcy hollered, "Call security!"

A woman stuck her head out of the eyeglasses store and waved. "I'll call. Are you okay?"

"Yeah." The shop's money bag had been hidden inside a FedEx envelope tucked safely under her arm. Had he taken that, too?

Darcy rushed out the door to chase the guy through the poorly lit parking lot, yelling for him to stop—as if that would really help.

With a glance over his shoulder, he made a quick cut between cars, banged into the hood of the vehicle, bounced off it like a pinball and then fell to the ground. He struggled to his feet, yanked open the purse and looked inside. In the distance, a mall security vehicle with a yellow flashing light appeared. The guy cursed and slung the purse aside. Then he took off so that she lost sight of him.

Car tires squealed somewhere out of sight. Apparently, he'd had someone waiting to pick him up.

As she ran to pick up her purse, she reached for her cell phone. It wasn't in her pocket. Hurrying back inside, she glanced around near the night deposit and found her phone on the floor. The

Optician employee held up the store's money bag to show she'd found it. At least the thief hadn't gotten that.

With shaking fingers, Darcy dialed 9-1-1 and reported the robbery. A minute later, mall security arrived.

All Darcy's belongings were found safely in her purse. Thankfully, she'd had the money bag disguised as a package, and the shop's money was accounted for. The whole time she was on the phone and talking with police, all she could think was how grateful she was that the security vehicle had pulled down her aisle at that moment. Grateful that the guy hadn't been armed, and that she hadn't been injured…or worse.

Thank You, Lord, for protection.

She hated to admit it, but Luke had been right.

I want him here with me. I need him.

Even if he said "I told you so." Even if he once again insisted she quit her mall job. Even if he dogged her every footstep for the next week.

The police took her statement, then the officers left to go examine security camera footage. Once the store's money was safely deposited, she made the dreaded call to her manager who, surprisingly, thanked Darcy profusely.

When she was finally free of her duties, Darcy dialed the person she most needed to talk to.

"Hey, Darcy, what's up?" Luke said.

Hearing his voice glued her mouth shut. Why had she called him? She shouldn't act like a needy wimp. After their kiss, he would fear she'd fallen for him or something. He'd think she was acting like every other female who'd ever wanted his attention.

And that would freak him out. He'd leave town so quickly she'd be left bobbing in his wake.

"Darcy? Are you there?"

Simply hearing the concern in his voice sent her throat to convulsing and nose to stinging. "I got robbed," she blurted in a pitiful, wimpy voice she hardly recognized.

"Where are you?"

She could imagine him with jaw clenched, color streaking across his cheeks, muscles coiled to act. The thought made her want to cry, now that the adrenaline had passed.

She cleared her throat before he went into full panic mode over her silence. "I'm okay. I'm at the mall entrance."

"On my way."

Less than fifteen minutes later, an indication he'd broken the speed limit, he charged into the mall, expression frantic, as if ready to slay dragons. The moment was the closest thing she'd ever had to experiencing a knight on a white horse.

When he spotted her sitting on the floor, back against the wall near the night deposit, he stopped in his tracks, fists clenching. His shoulders sagged, his relief was palpable even across that distance. She wanted to jump up and run into his arms.

She had no right. Their relationship was on rocky ground. Not to mention the kiss that he thought a mistake.

She had to get hold of herself. They needed to be able to work together for another week. Less than one week. Then he'd be happily on his way back to Tennessee. Away from her and what they could have had together.

Luke's knees nearly buckled when Darcy wiggled her fingers in a little wave, letting him know she was okay. Though he'd like to rage about her not taking his advice to get an escort, he quickly closed the distance, wanting to hold her in his arms.

How had he, even for one moment, thought he could sever his tie with her?

When she didn't stand and rush into his arms like he expected, he stopped and jammed his hands into his pockets to keep from reaching for her.

Yeah, they'd really messed up at the lake.

"Are you okay?" he asked, wanting to check her over yet unsure whether she would allow him.

She stood slowly, as if she might be injured. His heart lodged in his throat. "Did he hurt you?"

"No. I'm fine. He shoved me from behind, so my neck is a little stiff. Really, it wasn't as if he threatened me. No weapon. Just a grab and run."

"Just a grab and run? *Just?*" he nearly shouted. He paced to the door and back. "Darcy, please. You could have been hurt. Or worse. You have to quit this job."

"You know this isn't a dangerous job. We have security."

"And you haven't been taking advantage of that option when closing the store."

"I'll call security from now on. But I won't quit." She crossed her arms so stubbornly he didn't think he could manage another civil word.

Of course, she was right about the job being basically safe. At least compared to other jobs out there. Still… "Please consider quitting. You need to have time for a life, time to go out, to date, meet someone nice who deserves you. Someone you can spend your life with. Don't you want all that?"

She looked stricken, a shock of pain darting to her eyes.

"Look, I only meant—"

"I know what you meant. And I get it. Believe me I get it."

She didn't look at all as if she got what he was saying. She looked as if he'd stabbed her in the gut.

What did she want? For him to stay here, to beg his dad for a job and to attempt—and ruin—

a relationship with his best friend? "What do you want from me?" he asked, his voice strained and gravelly.

The pain in her eyes turned to steely, cool resolve. "Not someone telling me what to do. And certainly not that kiss."

"So we finally hit on the real issue. I already said it was a mistake. I'm sorry, okay? Can we move on?"

"Though I don't think it's possible to go back to the way things were, I believe we *can* be mature about it while we finish working on the auction."

He nodded. "Fine. Mature, it is."

"Fine." She nodded as firmly. Then winced as if it hurt.

He let out a huge sigh as he ran his fingers into her soft hair, massaging her neck muscles. "Look, I'm sorry. You know how I turn into a raving lunatic when I'm scared for someone I l—care about."

Love?

Had he really just thought that word?

His fingers froze momentarily, but then he resumed kneading her knotted muscles.

She remained stiff, as if she didn't want his touch. Gradually, she inched away, rolled her shoulders. "Thanks. I appreciate you caring."

Her gaze darted outside looking at something in the darkness. "I'm wiped out. Maybe later this week we can set up tables in the Fellowship Hall and then on Saturday take the auction items to the church."

"Sounds good."

She glanced outside again. "Good night." Yet she didn't make a move.

"I'm walking you to your car."

"Okay. No argument from me."

They walked in silence. When they arrived at her door, she reached for the handle.

"Wait."

She turned and leaned against the car, waiting for him to speak.

He had no clue what he'd wanted to say. He just didn't want her to leave so quickly.

Not a good sign. How was he going to leave after the auction?

Simple. He had a job to do in Nashville, people who happened to think he was good at that job. And he and Darcy had a friendship they needed to protect.

"Darcy, I really hate that a kiss is standing between us, like we always feared something like that might do. Please say you'll forgive me and try to move on."

"Why do you think it happened?" she asked instead, her gaze holding his as if something hugely important depended on his answer. "Honestly, Luke. Don't try to spare my feelings."

He couldn't tell her the whole truth. That the

kiss had cut him to the quick and left him raw, needing more from her than he'd ever dare ask. "I think that somehow, despite the fact that we grew up together, we're physically attracted."

She nodded, all business. "So that's it from your end? Improbable attraction?"

"Yes," he said immediately before he dared allow himself to tell her the crazy thoughts he'd been having. Thoughts about settling in Appleton, like his dad mentioned. Thoughts of seeing her every day. Of dating. All totally out of the realm of possibility if he was going to take over and run his new business in Nashville. "And you?" he had to ask as he, too, moved to lean against the car.

Her doelike eyes looking up at him in the moonlight made his heart thud in his chest. He reached for the ends of her long silky hair, brushing them between his thumb and forefinger gently enough that she wouldn't be able to feel it, the only closeness he could allow.

Why did he want to hold her close, anyway? To simply hug his good friend? Would those hugs even be possible anymore?

"I think feelings have no place in this discussion," Darcy said. "We know what we need to do."

No, feelings weren't relevant when he had a mortgage, a job commitment and the need to prove himself—if not to his dad, then at least to Roger and himself.

"Yep. Auction work," he said. "And then march toward our futures."

She looked up at him with a weak smile, then gave him a brief hug. "I guess I'll see you later this week. Good night, Luke. Thanks for coming when I called."

"Sure. That's what friends do."

She nodded and climbed into her car.

As she drove away, all he could think about was the feel of her arms around his waist and her hair brushing his chin in a hug that ended way too soon.

Chapter Ten

Feelings have no place in this discussion. No feelings. Feelings not allowed. To crush the memory of Luke charging in to rescue her last night at the mall, Darcy envisioned a big red circle with a line through it stamped over her feelings for Luke. She needed to focus on setting up for the auction.

"You are ridiculously stubborn, you know." Chloe lifted one end of the heavy eight-foot-long foldable, plastic table.

Darcy lifted the other end, and they carried the table across the church's small fellowship hall, placing it along the wall. They would have to squeeze in as many tables as possible to fit al the auction items. "One down, eleven more to go."

"I should have refused to come this late in the evening. Should have called Luke and told him what you're doing."

"I'm merely setting up tables to save him work

Plus, Grace has been sick this week with a stomach virus, so he's been staying with her. He took her to the doctor today, but she's still not better."

"You're avoiding him."

She glared at her sister as she scooted another table from the stack onto its side and unfolded the legs at one end. "I have every right."

Chloe opened the legs at her end, and they set the table on its feet. Then they hauled it to the opposite wall, sliding it in place by the first one. "Suppose you tell me what's going on. You've acted weird all week. And at church on Sunday, when Luke got within ten feet of you, you fled in the other direction."

"We kissed," she blurted, the announcement spewing like carbonation from a just-opened can of Coke.

She really needed to develop a better filter around her sister.

As if processing that bombshell, Chloe stared at her, shaking her head. Darcy had to give her credit, though. She didn't looked as earthshakingly shocked as expected.

"Now *that's* a development. And about time, I'd say."

Exactly what she suspected her sister would say. "No, it's *not* about time. The kiss was a disaster. After he looked forty-five shades of horrified, he called it a huge mistake." She crossed her arms and raised her brow. "Admit it. Not exactly what you'd want to hear after you kiss someone."

Chloe raised a brow to match Darcy's. "Did you force the kiss on him?"

"No. He initiated it." Her face burned as if she'd scooted too close to a Bunsen burner. "I may have closed the gap."

"Well, there you go. He was a willing participant. You don't make that kind of *mistake,*" she said, wiggling her fingers in quotation marks, "unless it's something you want."

"Participant or not, it doesn't matter now. He's avoiding me, too."

"So? Now you deal with the fact that you're more than friends. You can't ignore those feelings."

"Yes, we can." She grunted as she picked up another table. "We go back to acting as if everything is normal. Otherwise, what are our options? Acting like fools declaring our love and devotion on the phone from three hundred miles apart, and kissing each other at Christmas and Thanksgiving?" Her voice wobbled from saying the scary words she'd been thinking. "Oh, and then don't forget the part where I suffer a broken heart, just another of his conquests." Because, how likely was it Luke would suddenly decide to commit, would decide she was the right one for him? How was Darcy any different from Chloe and the others he dated?

There was no way for a relationship even if they wanted it, even if he wasn't such a poor risk. Darcy wanted to be near home and family and had a job she loved. Luke was determined to prove himself, to make his own way in Tennessee. He'd finally found the success he'd always wanted and wouldn't walk away from that.

They carried two more tables in silence, proving Chloe had no answer to the dilemma.

"Admit it," Darcy said. "You know how he never settles down. If a woman even hints at love or long-term, he can't get away fast enough. And I want long-term."

"I'm glad to hear it," said a man several yards away.

Darcy whirled around at the voice, nearly dropping the table, to discover who had heard her embarrassing admission.

"Who's the hunk?" Chloe whispered. Then she gasped in recognition.

As the handsome guy approached, Darcy realized it was Bryan. Days before she expected him. "Bryan?"

He smiled. "Thought I'd arrive early and surprise you."

"I'm glad you're here." As they hugged, she registered the huge change in his appearance since the last time she'd seen him on TV. "Look at you with a buzz haircut and beard. I hardly knew you, except for that big smile and your bright green eyes."

Darcy pulled her gaze away from Bryan's. "You may remember my sister, Chloe. Chloe, this is my high school friend—

"Bryan Winningham," Chloe blurted. "I'm a huge fan. Love your lyrics."

"He's come to save our auction," Darcy added.

With a friendly smile, he shook Chloe's hand. "Good to see you again, Chloe. Glad to know you're a fan."

Bryan scanned the room. "Your mom told me where you were. I'm here to help set up."

"That's so nice of you," Chloe said. "Because I need to go and hated to leave Darcy by herself."

What? Surely Chloe wasn't trying to play matchmaker. Darcy turned her face away from Bryan and widened her eyes at her sister. *What are you doing?*

"I'm sorry, Darcy. I totally forgot to mention that I needed to go back to the shop to close up."

Chloe, who not five minutes before had been pushing Darcy and Luke together, was now pushing Darcy on poor, unsuspecting Bryan?

Darcy would wring her neck later. "That's fine."

Chloe headed over to grab her purse from a table and winked at Darcy on the way out the door.

Not knowing what else to do, Darcy grabbed

another table. "We have a few more to set up. If you don't mind…"

"I'm happy to help."

As they lined up tables in the center of room, she found herself staring at him. He'd recently cut off the long, unruly blond hair that had hung in his eyes. Now it was close-cropped and darker. And the well-groomed beard made him look much older than the last time she'd seen him. He'd also filled out in the chest and arms, was much broader, more muscular.

Bryan really had ended up handsome. No wonder she'd heard that girls were going crazy for him at concerts.

Once the last table was set in place, they covered each with a white cloth.

"Do you have items to set up yet?" Bryan asked.

"Luke Jordan and I are going to do that on Saturday."

"So Luke's back in town, huh?"

"He's visiting, and helping on the auction."

"I see. I heard he finally settled down and made it through law school."

She wanted to defend Luke but recognized Bryan spoke the truth. "Yes. He's doing very well."

"Is he by any chance the man you were talking about when I came in?"

Darcy wanted to slink away and die of mortification. "Um. We've always been good friends."

He nodded. "So now it's more?"

"No!" she said too quickly and way too forcefully. "I mean, the relationship is mostly the same. Though it's been a little, um, different lately." Embarrassment scalded her face.

"I see. So, the same...yet different." Humor sparked in his eyes as brightly as his smile.

She had no idea what to say. She hadn't talked to Bryan in ages and certainly didn't plan to bare her soul. Instead, she pressed a cool hand to her cheek, hoping to tone down the hideous red she knew streaked across her pale skin.

"Ignore me," he said with a laugh. "I'm teasing you. Just say the word, and I can help on Saturday."

Straightening her T-shirt, she tried to act as if she hadn't just practically admitted she felt something for Luke. "Sure. We'd love some assistance. I'll call and let you know when and where."

They flipped off the lights and locked up. Bryan walked Darcy to her car.

"It really is good to see you again," he said. "I hate that I haven't been home in so long."

"I imagine you've been really busy."

He crossed his arms and leaned against her car, feet crossed at the ankle, as well. A pose she remembered well. Only back then he appeared to do it nervously. Now he looked confident and relaxed.

"I have been traveling a lot," he said, angling

toward Darcy, leaning closer. "But I should never get too busy to come see my friends."

Was he flirting? For some reason, her face grew hot. Surely, he didn't think she was flirting with him. Especially after their conversation inside. "I'm sure your mom and sister are glad to see you."

"Yes. They're glad you called me. *I'm* glad, too."

This was getting way too personal. "I appreciate the donation. You can bring those items with you on Saturday. And if you'd like, I can give you a receipt for your taxes."

"Sounds good."

She reached for the door handle, hoping he would move so she could leave before she embarrassed herself further.

He didn't budge. "Actually, I was hoping you would go out with me sometime while I'm here. That is, if you're not dating Luke or anyone else."

She nearly gasped. He *had* been flirting. "No, I'm not dating anyone. The thing with Luke, well, it's a little complicated. I can't lie about that. I've recently realized I may, um, have feelings for him."

"I understand. I'd like a chance to change those feelings."

She nearly swallowed her tongue. Managed to nod.

"How about tomorrow night?"

She couldn't go out with Bryan. Could she? "Well, um…I, uh, work tomorrow night at the mall. Friday night, too. I'm sorry."

"Saturday, then? After we finish setting up?"

Luke's words, telling her she needed to date and find someone nice, hammered through her mind. That, and the horrified expression on his face as he pulled away from their kiss.

This was a nice, talented, generous man standing here in front of her, looking at her as if he was genuinely interested. She'd be crazy to say no.

Besides, it could be one step in gaining her freedom. Freedom from the hold Luke had on her. "Okay, sure."

A slow, sweet smile slid across his face, and his emerald eyes lit. "I've wanted to hear you say you'd go out with me since high school. Even summers during college. Just never had the nerve to ask you. I look forward to it."

He opened her door and helped her inside. Polite, solicitous, successful…and cute. Someone even Luke would approve of.

Darcy truly did need to get out and enjoy life. This would be good for her, would help take her mind off what she couldn't have.

She'd have to do a lot of work on her attitude, though. Because despite Bryan's attributes, all she could think about was what if, instead of Bryan, Luke had asked her out?

* * *

"I'm admitting Mrs. Hunt to the ICU," the emergency room doctor said.

Luke's heart sank. "I thought it was the stomach flu. She's had intestinal symptoms, now fever, aches and chills."

"Yeah," Burt said. "That's what Grace's doctor told Luke yesterday."

"I suspect food poisoning and am afraid the infection may have spread. Appears to be some kidney involvement. We need to run more tests, get her stabilized. Why don't you two go up to the ICU waiting room until we get her settled?"

Ice ran through Luke's veins as he and his dad took the elevator to the second floor in silence. The small waiting room walls were lined with chairs littered with discarded newspapers and magazines. A utilitarian room that didn't offer much comfort to worried family members. A woman sat in the corner reading a book and barely gave them a glance as they entered.

Luke paced the floor, wishing he could call Darcy. She'd understand the medical jargon, might be able to tell them more about what was going on.

While Luke paced, his dad sat stoically, looking shell-shocked.

Please, Lord. Dad can't take more loss.

Word of Granny's arrival in the ICU didn't take long. He and Burt headed to her glassed-in room at the perimeter of the nurses' station. She was either sleeping or nonresponsive and looked frighteningly sick with her pale, clammy skin, hooked up to an IV and machines that beeped and whooshed.

Fear clawed at his insides. He reached for his phone and clicked on the one name he knew he could count on.

"Hello?" Darcy said.

"Granny's been admitted to the ICU."

A sharp intake of breath sounded on the line. "I'm on my way up."

He'd forgotten she would be at the hospital working. They'd had a rough night with Granny, and he'd lost track of time. At the moment, he was grateful to know Darcy was nearby.

Arriving a few minutes later, she slipped in the door.

Burt stood and ran a hand through his hair. "I'm going to grab some coffee and meet Noreen in the lobby." He'd been wild-eyed since they came in the room. Though he'd been with Luke's mom every minute of her illness, it had taken its toll. Burt didn't do hospitals well.

Once he left, Darcy scooted two chairs beside the bed and made Luke sit, then sat beside him. "Tell me what you know."

"She doesn't have the stomach flu. More likely food poisoning, and the infection has spread. Kidneys may be involved. They need to run tests."

"I checked before I came up here," she said. "They sent some cultures to the lab, including blood cultures. If anything grows, I'll be the first to know."

"So they think it could be in her blood? That's really serious, isn't it?"

"I'm sure they're following protocol. They'll look for anything and everything."

Luke could depend on her to keep him informed. And to do her job well. "I remember how frustrated you were to be a student when your dad was so sick, then got pneumonia. You felt you had no way of helping. Now here you are, in the right place at the right time to help Granny."

"It's the part of my job I love best." She stood and felt Grace's forehead, smoothed back her hair. "She's still feverish."

He got up and slid an arm around Darcy's waist. Took hold of Granny's soft hand, running his thumb over knuckles that felt dry, probably from dehydration.

Darcy's hands rested on the bed rail, clamped together so tightly her fingers were white at the knuckles. He worked his way between her hands so that he could take hold of one. "I'm encouraged, knowing you're watching out for her."

"I'll do everything I can on my end."

Having her nearby warmed the iciness that had rushed through his veins the moment the doctor had mentioned the ICU. "This sounds crazy, but I wish now I hadn't mentioned to her that I'd asked Dad to move."

"How did she react when you told her?"

"Said she wished I'd move back here, but then she was typical Granny, being supportive, telling me I could succeed on my own."

Smiling, Darcy smoothed the pillow beside his grandmother's head. "She loves you so much that you could do just about anything, and she'd think it was wonderful." She glanced at him over her shoulder. "So what did Burt say?"

"Said he wouldn't move, wouldn't want to start over in my practice."

Gazing at him in the semidarkness, her irises appeared nearly black. "Were you honestly surprised?"

"Actually, I was. Of course, I formed my plan when he was depressed and talking of moving. Noreen in the picture has changed his outlook."

She turned back to watch Grace.

He did the same, quiet, comfortable.

"I'm sorry I avoided you this week," she whispered. "Except for calling you after the robbery, of course."

Glad they could talk, could be friends again, he gave her shoulder a gentle squeeze. "I understand. I'm glad you showed up today. You didn't have to."

"Yes, I did. I love Grace, too."

She'd come purely out of concern for his grandmother. And maybe to support him as well, loyal to the core.

He was blessed to have a friend like Darcy.

Friends who kissed like they had?

The thought, unbidden, wouldn't leave his head, especially with her standing so close.

He stepped away, looking out at the nurses' station. Through the glass, Luke spotted Burt, Noreen and their pastor approaching.

"I need to go down to the lab," Darcy said. "I'll let you know if the cultures grow anything."

"Thanks. I'm glad to know you have my back."

After the mistake at the lake, Luke was glad they were once again on friendly terms. With Granny so sick, he needed that now more than ever.

The next day, Darcy and her coworker Lois checked Grace's cultures in the morning and again in the afternoon.

Nothing. No pathogens, nothing suspicious.

Helpless, Darcy had asked Lois to check one more time later in the day and to call if she discovered anything.

Darcy prayed for Grace as she cleaned the dark surface of the work area, the familiar smell of the bleach solution burning her nostrils.

Once she discarded her lab coat and vinyl

gloves, she washed her hands. Time to drive to Glitzy Glenda's for her shift there.

"Darcy, come look," Lois called from the back of the room.

"What is it?"

"I did another check of Mrs. Hunt's blood cultures like you asked and thought one bottle looked suspicious. I did a Gram's stain and found something strange."

Oh, no. Grace had been in the hospital for over twenty-four hours, and Darcy had hoped that by now they would have had at least a preliminary identification of the cause of her infection. But she certainly hadn't wanted to find the organism in Grace's blood.

Darcy hurried to the back of the lab where two microscopes were set up. Lois's big brown eyes shone with concern as she moved out of the chair and Darcy took her place. Peering into the eyepiece, she fine-tuned the focus to examine the stained slide.

She gasped when she discovered Lois had found something all right. "She has septicemia. The infection has gotten in her blood."

"Yeah. What is that organism, though?"

The bacteria *was* unusual. Darcy moved the slide to look at different areas. Something about the view under the microscope nagged at her, looked vaguely familiar…

"Oh, my goodness. Could it be?"

"You think you've seen this before?"

"Yeah, an organism on my final exam in Bacteriology class looked like this." Had Grace eaten tainted food? "This may be Listeria." Darcy's stomach twisted as she thought of the how the bacteria could kill those with weakened immune systems, could kill the elderly. Grace qualified in both cases.

"Listeria? We don't have the necessary equipment to identify that here."

"We'll have to send it off to the state reference lab." The thought made her sick at heart. Now they'd have to wait to identify the organism. "I'll call the results."

While Darcy pulled up Grace's specimen record on the computer, she jotted the results on paper. She might not be able to confirm anything, but the least she could do was tell the doc her suspicions, so he could make sure he was treating for the bacteria, just in case.

Darcy located the name of the physician and had him paged. She didn't have to wait long. When the doctor called the lab, she filled him in on their discovery, giving only the facts.

"Any idea what it could be?" he asked.

"All I can tell you officially is what I saw on the stain. Honestly, the organism looks familiar. Like something I identified in class."

"Tell me your suspicions."

Her heart pounded in her ears. What if she was wrong? "I can't say for sure, but it reminds me of Listeria."

He whistled. "You know, that would fit the history and symptoms. When can you have confirmation?"

She let out a pent-up breath. "We don't have the capability in a lab this size to identify the bacteria. Have to send it to the state, and that usually takes a while."

"Then I'll make sure Mrs. Hunt's antibiotic is effective against Listeria. If not, I'll add something that will be. At this point, I'm ready to try anything."

What if her guess was way off and it turned out to be some other strange organism? If only she could give him more information.

Listeria did have one unique characteristic, though. "You know, I might be able to rig up a test to give us more on the tentative identification. Unofficial, of course."

"Mrs. Hunt isn't improving, so anything you can do would help."

Darcy hung up the phone, stowed her purse and slipped back into her lab coat and gloves.

"What'd the doc say?" Lois asked.

"He's going to treat her for Listeria. I'm going

to see if I can come up with a test similar to one I used on my exam."

Lois grinned. "Great idea. But won't you be late for your mall job?"

Her boss wouldn't be happy, but the hospital took priority. The results could be critical. "This won't take me long. My manager will have to wait."

Darcy set up the makeshift test and then rushed out of the hospital. On the way to the car, she tried to call Luke to give him the news but got no answer. She sent him a text telling him his granny's cultures were positive and he could call or talk to the doctor.

When Darcy arrived at Glitzy Glenda's, her boss was at the shop entrance with her purse on her shoulder, ready to fly out the door.

"I'm sorry Mrs. Johnson. I had to set up a test for a very ill patient."

"This store depends on you, too. I'm sorry, but I'm putting you on warning for this tardiness and for calling in sick at the last minute."

"I understand." At the moment, Darcy didn't care. With Grace's health, Darcy had bigger things to worry about than a verbal warning. She would do whatever it took to help Grace, even if it meant losing this job.

Clocking in at the cash register, her heart ached

for Luke and Burt. How could they handle something happening to Grace?

With God's help. That was the only way to make it through times of struggle. Something Darcy needed to remember.

Lord, help me depend only on You. And please watch over Grace, heal her of this infection.

About an hour into Darcy's Friday night shift, the pre-teen and teen customers began to arrive in droves, distracting Darcy from repeatedly checking her phone for messages from Luke. She even had pretty decent sales after trying Chloe's tip to wear the jewelry herself. The move led to purchases, especially of the items she was wearing. She could only hope the sales success could help save her job.

A half hour before closing, the pretty redhead showed up wearing her pink pearls. With a new set of friends.

"Hi," the girl said shyly, her face radiating happiness.

A deep sense of satisfaction made Darcy feel like a proud big sister. "How's it going?"

"Great." Her eyes sparkled, and she appeared more relaxed than on previous visits.

"Are you enjoying your necklace?"

"I love it. Wore it to school today and got lots of compliments."

Darcy nodded as she straightened a stack of wallets. “I’m glad.”

“Actually, I came to thank you.” Her fair cheeks turned pink.

“For what?”

“For encouraging me to meet some new, nice friends.” She gestured toward two girls who were across the store looking at belts.

Pleased, Darcy gave a thumbs-up. “I’m really happy for you.”

“I’m just glad you were brave enough to basically do an intervention for an unhappy stranger.” She grinned and blinked away tears.

“Brave? Oh, I don’t think—”

“You didn’t have to say anything to me. You could have ignored all of us. Or just tried to sell your purses and jewelry.”

With a tentative smile, Darcy said, “I have to admit that’s what I did the first time you were here.”

“You didn’t the next time, though. You said something, and it’s changed my life. Thank you.”

Yet Darcy couldn’t have made that difference if Luke hadn’t urged her to step up. “Thanks. Good luck to you.”

Darcy felt like a fake. She was anything but brave. She wouldn’t have even spoken to the girl without Luke’s encouragement, and she often acted out of fear. Fear of being alone. Fear of being unable to support herself. Fear of never being loved the way she wanted to be loved.

She hadn't had the nerve to tell Luke her true feelings the whole time she was growing up, not until years after the fact.

And now? No way could she reveal that the crush had returned with a vengeance, that she'd poured her heart into their kiss. No, she was no role model. She'd been a flat-out coward where Luke was concerned.

Could she change that? Should she? Or were some things better left unsaid—especially when the heart was involved?

Chapter Eleven

"And thanks to Darcy O'Malley from the lab, we have at least a guess as to what's causing Mrs. Hunt's infection." The doctor stood at the foot of Granny's bed, flipping through the chart.

Darcy had information on Granny? Glancing at his phone, Luke found an unread text message from Darcy. He also had a missed call.

"What does she have?" Burt asked the doctor from the opposite side of the bed, his face weary.

"Earlier today, the blood cultures came up positive for bacterial growth."

Luke's heart lurched. "That can be deadly."

The doctor flipped another page over. "I won't lie to you. This is serious. But I think we can remain positive."

"What about treatment?" Burt asked.

"Ms. O'Malley thought the unusual organism looked familiar, but they're not equipped to identify it here. They have to send it to the state reference lab. Thanks to her sharp eye, I've added another antibiotic and think we're now on the right track for treatment."

Burt reached out and touched Grace, who stirred but remained too sick to open her eyes or respond. "How did she get it?"

The doctor scribbled something on the file. "Probably contaminated food." With a smack, he shut the file and slid it in its slot. "This infection is harder on the sick and the elderly. Let's pray the meds are effective. We really need to get her through the night."

Luke felt as if he was underwater trying to suck in air. "And if she doesn't get better tonight?"

"Like I said, I'm remaining positive. With the new antibiotic, I expect she should turn around soon."

Should. Luke wouldn't consider the alternative.

As soon as the doctor left the room, Luke stepped to the window and dialed Darcy.

"Is Grace okay?" she asked, a note of panic in her voice.

"No real change."

Darcy sighed, sounding drained. "Well, I guess that's good if she's not worse."

"I called to thank you. The doctor told us you gave a tentative ID on what's causing her infection."

"Yeah. If I'm right, then it's definitely a God

thing. I mean, what are the odds she would contract the exact same organism I had to identify on a final exam in school? And that I would recognize it by a Gram's stain?"

Humbled by how God was faithful even when Luke hadn't been, he said, "I'm thankful. We'll pray her through this."

"We will. I called the church, and they've already started the prayer chain."

"Thanks. You know, I'm grateful to you, too. You're one smart woman."

"We'll see if I'm right, hopefully by tomorrow if the test I rigged up confirms my suspicion."

Luke turned to lean his back against the wall and discovered his dad watching him.

Maybe he was talking too loud. "So you'll let us know?" he asked Darcy in a lower voice.

"Of course. As soon as I know anything."

He didn't want to hang up. Wished she could be there with him. "I'll see you tomorrow, to set up at the church?"

"Stay there with Grace. Bryan said he could do it."

Luke should be relieved. So why did anything having to do with Darcy and Bryan drive him half insane? "Okay. Tell Bryan I appreciate him helping you."

"Promise you'll let me know if anything changes

at the hospital? In the middle of the night, whenever, okay? I'll come if you need me."

"Thanks. I will."

He hung up and found his dad with his head leaning against the wall, eyes closed.

"Darcy said she'll call us if she knows anything more on the infection."

"I appreciate her diligence."

Luke stood over his grandmother rubbing her hand. *Lord, please give Darcy and the doctors answers, and please heal Granny's body. Lord, I've been a slacker for a while now. Help me be more faithful in worship and prayer. I want to do Your will.*

"So who's this Bryan?" Burt asked, startling Luke. "Noreen has mentioned him."

"A high school friend of Darcy's. He's actually become a successful musician and made a big donation for the auction."

"Generous of him. So why did you look so disgusted talking about him?"

He'd have to watch himself better. "Didn't mean to."

"A little of the green-eyed monster?"

Luke couldn't lie. His dad wasn't stupid. "It's complicated."

Burt gestured for him to have a seat. Luke pulled over a chair.

"You know, son, I've found that when we say things are complicated, they're usually very simple."

Luke shook his head and glanced away, fearing his dad would see the conflicted feelings that had been making him half crazy.

Leaning forward, forearms on his knees, Burt angled his head, locking gazes. "For instance, it should be simple to admit you've cared for Darcy your whole life. Simple to admit you light up when you're around her or talk to her. And though it may not be as simple to admit, it's obvious you feel more for her than friendship."

"Dad—"

"No, let me finish. Someone has to force you to face it. For whatever reason, neither you nor Darcy is able to acknowledge your feelings."

"I don't want to mess up again. I nearly lost her friendship when I dated Chloe and Raquel. I don't want to risk hurting Darcy and losing my friend."

"You won't lose your friend. You'll gain a lot more."

Mirroring his dad's posture, Luke stared at the floor. "I'm not good at committed relationships. She needs someone who'll treat her like she deserves to be treated, a good guy like Bryan."

"You've never had a relationship with someone

you cared about so much. How do you know you won't be good with Darcy?"

Luke had never been perceptive enough to notice she had feelings for him. Apparently, he was a clueless fool. She deserved the perfect man, the perfect relationship, like she'd always dreamed of. Her perfect Prince Charming.

He was certainly no Prince Charming.

"Dad, I appreciate your concern, but I know what I'm doing. Besides, I have my new life in Tennessee."

Squinting, Burt leaned back, crossed his arms over his chest and examined Luke. "You've surprised me, you know. When you started law school I wondered if you could stick with it and succeed. I owe you an apology for that."

Luke had waited a long time to hear those words. He nodded, pleased for the recognition. "Thanks."

"I know I'm not good at saying how I feel, but I'm learning."

"Noreen?"

"Yes, in fact, she's been teaching me to open up. Has taught me a lot about myself. And…" He hesitated.

For the first time in years, Luke felt a sense of closeness to his father. "And?"

Burt looked up, concerned. "I'm going to ask her to marry me."

Luke felt as if he'd been slammed against the back of his chair. For some reason, though, the thought didn't seem as out of the question as it would have two weeks ago.

"Wow," was all he could manage to say.

"I know it's quick. But one thing I've learned," he said, nodding toward Grace, "is we need to live in the present. Not waste a precious moment of time."

Thinking of his mother's battle with cancer, and now Granny's illness, Luke knew his dad was right.

Burt put his hand on Luke's shoulder. "I want you to know I'll always love your mother. I've told Noreen that, and she wouldn't have it any other way."

Luke nodded, his throat tight. He felt a sense of relief to know Dad hadn't just marched ahead with a new life, pushing Mom into the past. "I appreciate you telling me that."

"We both miss Joan and talk about her often."

Luke looked into his father's eyes, eyes that matched his. "I miss her so bad, and I still feel guilty that I didn't come home more often while she was sick."

"Son, she didn't want you leaving school."

"But I should have come, anyway. When she told me not to, I should have insisted."

"Your mom was proud of how you buckled down in college, how you worked and achieved your dreams. She wanted you to push ahead, to make your way without her health holding you back."

Working for that law degree, though, had been about more than simply achieving his dream. "I was determined to be successful, to prove you wrong." Luke gave his dad a sad smile. "I'm afraid I put that desire before mom. And now, I look at my decision to stay in Tennessee after graduation, and wonder if that was a mistake. Because every time I'm home, I regret it. Sometimes, I wish I had come here instead."

Burt reached out and put a hand on Luke's arm. "Son…"

"Then I feel more guilty, because if I decided to come back to Appleton now, then staying in Nashville away from Mom was done in vain."

Shaking his head, Burt's brow drew down in concern. "No, your time in Nashville was good for you. I see a big change in your confidence. Your mom was right in suggesting I not offer you a partnership right out of law school."

Luke stilled. Shook his head, thinking surely he hadn't heard correctly. "Are you saying that's why you never asked me to join you? Not because you thought I wasn't capable?"

"Of course you're capable. Once you stuck with law school and did well, I knew, with your people skills, you'd be a good attorney. But your mom was afraid, with all those job offers you had, that you'd settle for coming home just because of her illness."

Leaning his head back, Luke let out a sigh. "I can't believe this. I totally misunderstood. Was hurt you didn't ask."

"Luke, I'm sorry. Joan and I assumed if you really wanted to move home you'd feel free to ask. Then you called, so excited about the other offers…"

He looked at his dad, with the monitors beeping in the background, the sounds of nurses hustling around outside the door, and knew this was a big moment. But a difficult moment nonetheless. "I've never wanted anything more than to have an office beside you and a sign with both our names out front."

"Then do it. Join me as partner. In a few years, I want to semiretire to spend more time with Noreen. Down the road, the practice would be yours."

Luke had waited as long as he could remember to hear those words. Ever since he was barely old enough to read and sat at his dad's desk, playing with the pens and pencils, trying to read huge law books, sounding out hard-to-pronounce words.

"I know you've done well with Roger and are committed to him. But promise me you'll at least consider my offer," Burt said, looking hopeful, pleased.

"I will."

"And remember, Noreen and I both love you. I hope you can be happy for us."

"I am happy for you."

His dad's forehead wrinkled, lifting his brows in doubt.

"I truly am."

Joy filled Burt's eyes as he reached through the bed railing to smooth Grace's blanket. "Lately, I've learned to appreciate what's right in front of me. I hope you will, too."

Luke's neck heated up. Was Dad talking about Darcy?

"I know what's rattling around in that head of yours." Burt leaned back in his chair, crossed his arms over his chest and smiled.

"That I just bought a building and leaving Nashville would be complicated?"

"You're thinking about Darcy." He leaned closer. "Don't miss out on love simply because you've known her your whole life. Or because you think you're not good at commitment. When the timing and the person are right, you'll be perfectly able to commit. Like you committed to law school and proved me wrong."

Ideas exploded in Luke's mind. So many possibilities. Possibilities he'd never dared imagine.

An offer making Jordan & Jordan a reality.

A wife—with long auburn hair and deep blue eyes, and two or three kids who looked exactly like her.

Antsy, Luke moved to the window and stared at the darkening sky. His dad made him reconsider dreams from childhood. Made him want things. Crazy, impossible scenarios he shouldn't want.

Remember Chloe.

No. He refused to remember Chloe.

Yet he had to be careful. He had to be certain about his feelings for Darcy. Had to know without a doubt that he could change, could take a step forward in their relationship without hurting her down the road.

For now, he would keep his dad's job offer to himself and focus on Granny and the auction.

"I don't believe it." Darcy let loose a loud whoop that ricocheted off the lab equipment on Saturday morning as she stood in the hospital lab and peered at the test tube. She handed the tube to Lois. "Check it out."

Lois held it up to the light and stared at the

bacteria's faint umbrella-shaped growth pattern. "It worked!"

"Yeah. I'm relieved." Relieved she hadn't made a mistake in giving the doctor a tentative ID.

Her risk had paid off.

Once she'd called the results to him and packed up the organism to send to the state lab, she headed upstairs to the ICU to check on Grace.

As Darcy barreled through the waiting room doorway, she discovered Luke, alone in the room, slouched in a chair with his head tilted forward and eyes closed. He was either asleep or praying.

Facing his piercing brown eyes and strong, square jaw sometimes required fortitude, so finding him resting proved a nice change. She approached, itching to brush back the hair that had fallen over his forehead. As she dragged her attention back to his face, golden-brown eyes met hers.

Her heart slammed against her ribs. "Oh, you're awake," she stammered, her face burning at being caught staring.

"Good morning." Beard stubble and messy hair gave him a dangerous look. Dangerously appealing.

"It worked." Unable to contain her excitement, she laughed at his look of confusion. "The test we rigged up unofficially confirmed the organism is what I suspected. How's Grace?"

He stood and rubbed the back of his neck.

"That's great news. The doctor did rounds early this morning, and Granny's shown marked improvement."

"So he thinks she'll recover?"

A devastating smile revealed even, white teeth. "Yes. And she was awake and talking by midmorning."

Darcy gasped and hugged him. "I'm so glad."

He wrapped his arms around her like old times. Comfortable. Not electrically charged like they'd experienced lately. Maybe they'd be okay after all.

"They're bathing Granny now," he said. "Dad's at lunch but will be back soon."

Mesmerized by the close proximity and his perfectly shaped, full lips, Darcy forced her gaze upward. This closeness was not going to be as easy as she'd thought. But she had to learn to handle being around Luke.

She could do this. She'd already taken a big step toward moving forward—the upcoming date with Bryan.

"Well...uh...tell Grace I'm thinking of her. If... you know...if she's still awake, I mean."

"Thank you."

"For what?"

"For the diagnosis, of course. I love how unassuming you are."

When he was so close, she felt like spiderwebs clung to her brain. Better he think her unassuming rather than addled. "Oh, that. I'm just thrilled that she's getting better." She stepped away from him so she could concentrate. "I should go."

"Oh, sure." He took a step away, as well. "But first, I wanted to tell you Dad and I had a good talk last night. Cleared the air."

"Good. I'm proud of you both for doing that." She couldn't help but wonder, though, whether they talked any more about working together—either in Appleton or Nashville. "So you feel you understand each other better?"

"Yeah, we both opened up. Talked a lot about Mom and Noreen. I feel like we're on solid ground."

Possibilities ran rampant in her mind. Apparently, Luke thought it wasn't Darcy's business. She had to respect his wishes. "I'm happy, then."

He raked a hand through his hair. "I know I'd normally tell you everything we said. I can tell you more about the conversation later. But I have a lot to think about, some decisions to make first."

Her heartbeat pounded in her ears. "Okay, thanks." She gave a tentative laugh. "I admit, I was wondering."

"I figured." He smiled, pushed her hair back from her shoulder. "Our relationship has changed, but we'll figure it out."

She nodded, her throat aching. Yes, they were both moving ahead and would eventually adjust.

That didn't make the in-between time easy. "Guess I'll see you at church tomorrow."

"Like I said, Dad will be back to the hospital soon to sit with Granny. I can help set up for the auction."

"Oh, okay. That'll be great. Come to my house when you finish up here."

He brushed a stray hair off her cheek, so nonchalantly that she didn't think he realized he did it. "I'll be there."

She stood rooted in place, not wanting to leave, as if they could just stand there and pretend their lives were back to normal. Yet, like it or not, everything had changed with that kiss.

"One more day until the auction is over," he said with a gentle smile. "Then your life will go back to normal."

Once again, he spoke her thoughts, the two of them in tune with each other. "Yep. Yours, too." She returned his smile and then slipped out of the waiting room. How in the world would she ever let Luke leave? How would she ever get over loving him?

"Oh, no," Darcy said that afternoon as she carried an armload of auction donations from her dad's office to her car.

Luke closed his now-full trunk. "What's wrong?"

"I forgot to let Bryan know when and where to meet us."

Luke knew he should not feel irritated Bryan would join them. "He can meet us at the church in a half hour or so."

"Good idea." She pulled out her phone and typed a text message, her fingers flying across the screen.

A moment later, a return message made a plinking sound. She read it and smiled. Then another little plink, and a new one made her laugh.

"Is that still Bryan?"

"Yes." She looked up at Luke, her beautiful freckled face so happy and carefree. Cheeks pink from exertion or from the scintillating text conversation?

"So he's meeting us at the church?" Luke asked.

"Actually, he's coming now to help you with the basketball hoop. I'd told him about it on Wednesday when he helped set up tables."

Helped set up tables? "I thought we were doing that today."

Her gaze darted away. "Chloe and I went ahead and met Wednesday to set up. When Bryan got to town, Mom told him where we were, so he came on over."

"Oh. I would have helped."

"You were taking care of Grace, so I just called Chloe when I happened to have an unexpected evening off. I think my manager felt guilty that I got robbed during her shift."

"Speaking of, have they caught the guy?" He

grabbed a heavy picture frame as she reached for it. "I'll get that."

"No luck. The security video was too grainy to tell anything."

"I'm sorry." He started to reach for her but instead tucked his hand safely in his pocket.

She was so beautiful, more beautiful than he'd ever realized. Of course, he'd always appreciated her inner beauty.

The conversation with his dad ran through his head, the possibilities so tempting. She'd make some man very happy someday. Would it be Luke? Or someone else?

As if summoned by the thought, a car pulled up in front of the house and slowed to a stop.

Drummer boy.

"Man, that was quick," he muttered.

"He lives on Pine Place."

Only two streets over. Lucky me.

Darcy waved at Bryan, but she didn't hurry down the front steps to greet him. Luke caught himself smiling. Stifled a chuckle.

Maybe Darcy was nervous. Or maybe she felt awkward with all of them together.

Torn loyalties?

When Darcy finally went down the sidewalk to greet Bryan, he gave her a hug and chaste kiss on the cheek. She did lean in, so maybe it wasn't so casual after all.

Bryan certainly looked pleased to see her, his grin flashy enough it could light up a stadium.

The drummer dragged himself away from Darcy long enough to turn the showbiz smile on Luke. "Good to see you again, Luke."

Luke joined them and shook his hand, trying not to let his agitation show. "Good to see you, too. Thanks for helping us."

Wasn't this exactly what he deserved? Hadn't he told Darcy she should find a man who could love her and make her happy?

"If you two can load the carton from the sporting goods store into the back of my car, I'll grab the last of the small items," Darcy said.

Luke motioned Bryan inside the garage. Each took hold of one end of the large box and headed to Darcy's SUV.

"So, Luke, I hear you're in Nashville now. I'll be moving up there before long."

"Yeah, Darcy mentioned it. Congratulations on your success."

"Thanks. Everything has been pretty crazy since we signed with the record label. My head hasn't stopped spinning. I feel blessed, though."

"I imagine your life has changed a lot," Luke said.

Darcy stood by the car and guided the box inside. "Yep, now he's got all the screaming fans."

"Oh, I don't know about that," Bryan said. "I'd be happy to impress one particular fan."

Luke froze. He looked from Bryan, who had a teasing glint in his eyes, to Darcy, whose face looked ready to go up in flames.

Blushing aside, she looked as if his comment pleased her.

Luke couldn't resist asking, "So, is there something going on between you two?"

"Luke." Darcy's tone admonished him for his comment even as she suddenly became very absorbed in reorganizing a box of crocheted items.

"I hope so." Bryan laughed, clapping Luke on the back as if they were the best of buddies and that Luke would understand.

Luke didn't understand. Not one bit. Did that mean Bryan had declared his interest but Darcy was resisting?

He pondered the situation all the way to the church and watched them like a hawk while they unloaded, staying close, alert to every word.

Once they unloaded the vehicles, Darcy took over. She had everything numbered and had a system for the display. Each item had a bid sheet with a description and minimum bid.

"Darcy, you've been working on this a lot more than I realized," Luke said. "I don't know when you found the time."

She shrugged. "I've done it before. Your mom taught me."

As soon as she said it, she laid her hand on his arm, a butterfly of a touch for comfort. She didn't have to say anything. She knew reminders of his mother's absence still hurt.

Darcy quickly continued directing him and Bryan, organizing and labeling recently donated items.

"Bryan, I plan to lock your items and a few other valuable ones in the storage closet," Darcy said. "I'll display them tomorrow after church."

"They're in the car. I'll get 'em." He strode out of the fellowship hall letting the door bang shut behind him.

Luke leaned against the door jam of the closet Darcy had opened. "What's the deal with you two?"

She busied herself clearing space on a table inside the dark closet. "I don't know what you mean."

Shaking his head, he chuckled. "Yes, you do."

Darcy stilled, palms flat on the table, her back curved as if someone had knocked the air out of her. He stepped up behind her and put his hands on her shoulders. "Darcy—"

"Don't." She took two quick breaths. "Let it go."

They weren't the same as before. He couldn't just jump into her business. "Yeah, I know."

"I'm doing what I need to do to move on from the *mistake* at the lake." She said the word as if it were nasty and hateful.

He'd thought they'd moved past that night. "I'm sorry if what I said hurt you."

She turned so quickly he didn't have time to step away. Which put her in his arms facing him, looking up, so close he could lean down mere inches to touch his lips to hers again.

"What I want to know," she said, "is if you're sorry you kissed me."

He was sorry he messed everything up. Sorry he'd hurt her. Sorry he'd let himself fall for the fantasy they could have something more between them before he'd considered the consequences. But sorry for that amazing kiss? "No."

There. He'd admitted it. The honest, awful truth.

She staggered backward, breaking away from his arms, which he'd unwittingly wrapped around her waist. "Are you kidding me? How can you say that when you reacted so strongly, so negatively?"

The door to the fellowship hall banged as Bryan came back inside. His footsteps sounded on the tile floor as he crossed the room toward the closet.

"I'm going out with him tonight," she whispered, her eyes flashing in the semidarkness. "I said yes."

He swallowed. Nodded. "It's what you should

do. He appears to be a good guy who appreciates you. You could be happy."

"Yeah, I could be. He really likes me, has had a crush on me since high school. And now, he's come charging in like the Prince Charming I always imagined."

Luke didn't think a knife between the ribs could hurt more than his chest hurt at the moment. From loss, disappointment. But more, from the sadness in her eyes.

How could she be talking about her Prince Charming charging in and not be lit up with happiness? *Have I done that to her?*

He tore his eyes away from hers before he said something he'd regret. He still needed time to figure out his own feelings. "I'll leave you two to finish up."

Holding a large box and a guitar case, Bryan nodded. "It was good to see you again, Luke. I hope to spend more time with Darcy, so I'm sure I'll see you again soon."

Luke backed out of the closet, making room for Bryan and his auction items. "I've got to go back to the hospital. See you both tomorrow."

He strode toward the door to the fellowship hall. He needed to get out of there.

Before exiting, he turned back to find Bryan standing outside the storage room showing Darcy an autographed guitar. His hand brushed Darcy's as she admired the instrument, and an awestruck smile spread across his face. The man was obviously crazy about her.

"Hey, Winningham," Luke called.

Bryan looked up.

"Be good to my best friend, or you'll have me to deal with."

"Got it." He gave a little salute, then went into the closet with the other items he'd donated.

Darcy deserved someone who could go all in. Someone who would do the love thing well.

Could Luke be that person? In Darcy's own words, he had left a wake of broken hearts behind him. Including hers.

He truly cared for her, but was that the kind of love that lasted?

He had to make sure he wasn't acting out of jealousy over Bryan or out of selfishness.

God, show me what I feel is true. Take away my selfishness and jealousy. And my pride.

Am I the one for Darcy, the one who can make her happy?

Despite how much Luke loved her, he wasn't sure.

Chapter Twelve

"Big sis to the rescue for your date tonight!" Chloe stood in Darcy's bedroom doorway with an armload of garments on hangers and a huge shopping bag from her boutique.

Darcy ushered her inside and shut the door. "Bless you. You don't know how much I appreciate your help."

"You sounded desperate."

"Definitely desperate. You've seen my wardrobe, ninety percent khaki and ten percent athletic apparel. Nothing appropriate for a first date with a budding celebrity."

Chloe dropped the bag filled with shoes and other accessories. She laid the clothes on the bed and picked up the hangers one by one. "Holler when you see something you like."

"I like that...and that..." One after another, Chloe presented something beautiful. "And that..."

Darcy had never seen so many gorgeous clothes, so perfect for her. "I can't possibly choose."

"You have to pick one. Where's Bryan taking you?"

She paused, wracking her brain. "He never said."

"Then we'll do something flexible." Chloe set aside the fancier dresses.

Darcy reached out with longing, touched a strap on a black cocktail dress. Ran her fingers over the elegant fabrics.

She yearned to put on the lacy cream-colored dress. The type of dress she always feared Luke and others would think didn't suit her because it was so feminine.

"I'm surprised you brought such frilly dresses for me," Darcy said, half afraid of Chloe's opinion.

"I know it's not your usual. You'd look great in any of these."

Bryan wouldn't remember her tomboy ways. He wouldn't think she was trying to be someone she's not. "Then I want to wear the cream lace one. Even if he takes me bowling or to a movie."

Chloe squealed and gave her a quick hug. "I'm so glad. I've wanted to see you in this for ages. The dress screamed your name as soon as I saw it."

Darcy wouldn't question her sister's opinion. She wanted to dress up and feel like a princess.

Over the next hour, Darcy felt like one. The

dress fit perfectly, as if the tailor made it for her athletic figure. Chloe fixed her hair in a loose bun with wisps of curls around her face. Then she applied soft, romantic makeup, a bit more than Darcy was used to yet tasteful.

"I can't believe you're so into this," Darcy said. "You were pushing me toward Luke as if you thought he was the man for me."

Chloe's expression sobered. "You deserve to feel pretty and appreciated. I just want you to be happy." She placed a bobby pin to hold an escaped section of hair. "I've always admired your smarts, your drive. Always wanted to be you when I grew up. But you've never had the confidence to go for the man of your dreams."

Darcy couldn't believe her sister was saying such things. She'd never realized any of it. "Chloe, I—"

"No, listen to me a minute. Luke or Bryan would be lucky to get you, and you need to keep that in mind when you're around them. Luke, especially, should appreciate you more."

Chloe smiled but didn't say anything else about Luke as she sprayed two puffs of hairspray to hold the tendrils in place. Once she pronounced the new look complete, Darcy headed to Chloe's childhood bedroom to stand in front of the full-length mirror inside her sister's closet door.

Before her was the image of the young woman

she often felt inside but had never seen in her reflection. "Wow. Is that really me?"

"Yep. You look stunning."

Not a word she would ever associate with herself. "From now on, I won't hesitate to wear something frilly or feminine. Everyone will simply have to adjust to the new Darcy."

Laughing, Chloe put an arm around her shoulder and squeezed. "Come on, Darcy, you've outgrown the tomboy phase. You're a beautiful woman now. Not only that, you're intelligent and successful. You deserve a great guy who knows what a catch you are."

Darcy hugged her sister and fought the lump in her throat. "I don't know how to thank you."

"I'll send you a bill." She winked. "Now, I've got to go. Have a wonderful time tonight."

Following her sister downstairs, Darcy tried not to tumble off the high heels. Once Chloe left, she went to switch her wallet and tube of lip balm—correction, pink lip*gloss,* to a ritzy new handbag. As she tucked her phone inside, she battled thoughts of Luke. Of the look on his face yesterday evening inside the storage closet.

He appeared upset that she'd accepted Bryan's invitation, yet he hadn't asked her not to go. He didn't care enough to step in, to stop her.

The doorbell rang, and she huffed, exasperated

that she thought of Luke at all on her big night out. Her princess night.

She approached the door as smoothly as she could in pumps, and paused to take a deep breath to calm herself before opening the door. A quick glance in the foyer mirror sent a thrill through her. She felt beautiful. Should feel confident.

He's only Bryan, my co-nerd from high school. Not Bryan the up-and-coming country music star.

As she opened the door with a smile on her face, she silently repeated, *He's only Bryan...*

Bryan stood on the doorstep, hands in pockets, staring at his feet. When he looked up, he sucked in a breath. "Wow. You're gorgeous."

"Thanks. You, too."

He laughed.

"I mean not gorgeous, but, well..." He did look so very handsome in khaki pants and a nice navy blazer, his beard freshly trimmed, smelling like a million bucks. She laughed. "Actually, you do look gorgeous."

A smile lit his face, his emerald eyes sparkling. "I have a feeling this is going to be a good night. You ready?" He offered his elbow.

She quickly locked the door and hooked her arm through his. "Definitely ready." Ready to move on with her life. To let go of Luke and his indecisiveness. "Where are we going?"

"A restaurant I've always wanted eat at, part of the Woodlands Resort."

"How nice. I love that place. It's—" A sleek black limousine sat in the driveway. In *her* driveway. "What in the world?"

A uniformed driver nodded and opened the door. "Good evening."

The smile didn't leave Bryan's face as he tucked her into the car, sliding in beside her. "At the time I planned this, I thought it was a great idea. Now it feels kind of awkward."

"I think it's wonderful," she said—admittedly giddy. "I've never ridden in one."

His cheeks reddened as he turned to face her and looked into her eyes. "Neither of us went to prom, and I never got the nerve to ask you, so I was hoping to make up for that."

Her heart thumped, not the kind of pounding or soaring that it did with Luke. But it definitely thumped. Maybe a good sign? "Thanks, Bryan. That's sweet."

He nodded and slid back against the seat, his gaze remaining on her.

Darcy peered out the window as they passed through downtown Appleton. Heads turned, people stared.

"I forgot what a scene this would make since it's not prom night. I'm sorry if you're embarrassed," he said.

A giggle escaped, and she wished she could snatch it back so he wouldn't realize how silly and grand she felt. "Hey, the windows are tinted. They don't know it's us."

Bryan scooted toward her and rested his arm on the back of the seat. A respectful distance remained between them, yet she felt crowded as he smiled and looked at her as if she was important, interesting, worthy of his full attention.

"I'm glad you came tonight," he said. "Glad to have this chance to take your mind off Luke."

"I've looked forward to it." She couldn't say he'd taken her mind off Luke, though. At least not yet. His piercing green eyes seemed to pry into her thoughts, so she looked away, afraid he'd read her hesitancy.

Darcy's heart lurched as she spotted Luke on the curb out in front of his dad's office, staring at the limo as it passed by. She could tell he was trying to see inside.

Does he know it's us?

She snapped her attention back to her date, the man who cared enough to ask her out, to treat her to a special night.

Bryan reached out his hand as if he was going to touch her face or hair, but then snatched it away. "I have to admit, this is difficult...not to push you or force something you're not feeling."

"Let's just enjoy the evening together and not worry about Luke or anything else, okay?"

His eyes lit with pleasure. "Okay."

And they did just that as they drove along the curvy mountain road to the Woodlands resort about thirty miles outside of town. The driver dropped them in front of the lodge, which housed one of the nicest restaurants in the area.

Of course, Darcy had never been there with a date. She'd only been to the lodge for a church women's retreat. But she'd heard about the romantic dining room for honeymooners. Had read about the elopement package the resort offered—had daydreamed about being whisked away to a tiny mountain cabin with a new husband...with unmanageable brown hair and golden-brown eyes.

A man who needed to be forgotten.

Pushing away thoughts of those brown eyes as they had watched the limo drive by, she stepped inside the restaurant. "It's beautiful."

A hostess greeted them, and the young woman's eyes nearly bugged out of her head when she saw Bryan's face. Glancing at the reservation book, she said, "I thought it was a joke."

"Pardon me?" Bryan said.

"I'm sorry." She blinked a few times and bit her lip to control the grin, as if trying to pull herself together and act professional. "Right this way, Mr. Winningham. Your table is ready."

Darcy fought her own grin at the surreal experience. She truly did feel like a princess on the arm of a celebrity.

They were escorted to a private dining room that had one whole wall of windows with a gorgeous mountain view, perfect sunset included. "Wow." *Oh, my goodness. A private dining room?* "This is spectacular," she said in a voice much calmer than she felt at the moment.

He pulled out her chair for her. "I hope you like it. I used to wait tables here on the weekends. Always thought I'd like to bring you here."

Darcy's insides warmed. "I'm touched you thought of me. I only wish I'd known back then."

Seated across from her, he leaned closer, laying his hand on top of hers. It felt odd to touch someone's hand besides Luke's. Not bad, just…strange. Comfortable.

Not nearly as thrilling.

"I hate that I never had the nerve to go after what I wanted back in high school. But I do have the nerve now. And I know exactly what I want." Heat lit his gaze, like the heat she'd witnessed in Luke's eyes. Only the heat went one way in this case. No zipping and zapping electrical current from her end.

Her heart sank. *Luke has ruined me for others. For now, anyway.*

Darcy smiled and gave his hand a quick squeeze before releasing it. "Let's enjoy a nice dinner. I'm starving."

With a crooked smile, he leaned back in his chair somewhat deflated. "I'm sorry I pushed. I'll back off until you give me the green light."

"Thanks, Bryan. It may take a little while."

He opened his menu. "Totally understandable. But promise you'll let me know if I'm totally out of the running. Don't want to make a nuisance of myself."

Nodding, she opened her menu. "You're never a nuisance. We'll always be friends."

And so went the rest of the evening. He was a wonderful dinner partner, great conversationalist, totally engaging, asking her about herself and her family.

Yet her heart wasn't in the date.

Her heart was in Appleton with the guy next door.

Later, as the limo pulled up in front of Darcy's house, Bryan turned toward her, lifted her chin to look into her eyes. "Did you have a good time tonight?"

"I had a lovely time. Thank you for the prom I never had."

Bryan gave her a tender, understanding look. "I think I can manage to stay in Appleton another night if you'll go out with me again after the auction tomorrow."

Darcy tried to smile, but the smile wobbled. "I'm sorry, Bryan. I can't go out with you again."

"Because of the complicated thing with Luke?"

"Yeah. You're a great guy, and I know I would enjoy spending time together. But my heart would be elsewhere."

"So I can't change your mind?"

She shook her head. "I'm afraid not. I'm sorry."

"Don't be. I'm glad I finally gave it a shot. Nothing ventured, nothing gained."

The exact phrase she'd said to Luke the night she called Bryan to ask for the donation. "I'm sure you'll find a great woman someday."

"Yeah, maybe in Nashville." He gave her hand a squeeze. "Hang in there. You'll figure it out."

"I hope so."

"I know so." He opened the car door and helped her out, settling her arm through his, then walked her to the front door.

She opened the door and faced him. "Thanks again."

He wrapped her in a friendly hug and kissed her cheek. "Hey, don't let him yank you around, being all wishy-washy. Promise me you'll hold out for total commitment."

No matter what Luke did, Darcy deserved total

commitment. Because when she finally made her own commitment, it would be for always. "I promise."

"Darcy, tell him how you feel. And if it doesn't work out, call me. I'll help pick up the pieces."

She gave him a pained look. "Bryan."

With a gentle, sad smile, he said, "It's what I do best—granted, usually in song lyrics. But I'd love the opportunity to try."

If only she could return his feelings. Surely, she was crazy for turning away this handsome, nice, talented man.

Bryan's bright smile gleamed in the porch light as he gave her a thumbs-up and headed back to the limo.

Before he could shut the door, she called out, "I'll still see you tomorrow at the auction, won't I?"

"Of course. No hard feelings."

Darcy couldn't believe she was sending such a wonderful, caring man away.

Then again, she couldn't believe she'd never truly gotten over Luke, either.

Someday in heaven she would ask God why He created her to love the one man she couldn't have.

Darcy's cell phone vibrated. Her heart jolted when she saw the text message was from Luke.

Impressive limo. Did you have a good time?

* * *

Luke stared at the text message he'd just sent Darcy, suddenly wishing he hadn't sent it. After a couple of minutes without a response, he especially regretted it.

She'd definitely arrived at home, though. The limo had just left. Maybe Darcy was ignoring him. Or maybe Bryan had stayed.

He tossed his phone on the counter. It vibrated, and he snatched it back up.

Darcy had answered his text. A very nice time.

Luke's gut tanked. He quickly typed a response. Did he ask you out again?

Yes.

His heart thunked in his chest. Why couldn't he be sure of his feelings? Why couldn't God knock him over the head with a clear answer? He was terrified he'd mess up with Darcy. What if she was the one for him, and he piddled around and missed his chance?

But what if he rushed into something and it ended up *he* wasn't the one for *her?*

Staring at her answer, he knew he had to do something. He typed, Can I come over?

An agonizing minute later, the phone finally vibrated.

I'll be on the patio.

A smile slid over his face as he strode out the door. He stepped around the corner of Darcy's house and stopped in his tracks. With waves of curls cascading around her face, Darcy stood watching for him, glowing in the moonlight like a vision in cream-colored lace. He sucked in a breath. "Darcy?"

Darcy bristled. He had to ask who she was? As if an elegantly dressed woman standing in front of him at this address could be someone else? "Hey. How's Grace doing tonight?"

"What?" He seemed distracted, but then his eyes snapped to her face. "Oh. Granny. She's doing even better this evening."

A rush of relief passed through her, followed by irritation that he seemed shocked by her appearance.

"You look beautiful," he said.

"Thanks." Her pulse thudded in her ears as she glanced away, unable to hold his gaze.

Indicating the glider, he ushered her into the seat as if she were breakable. A flutter tickled her chest.

He wedged in beside her trying not to bump her shoulder. "So you had a good time, huh?"

"Yes, we had a lovely dinner at Woodlands Resort."

He nodded. Crossed his arms. "And in a limo."

"Yes, the prom date neither of us got to experience. Bryan's very thoughtful."

Luke's jaw twitched. "So he asked you out again, huh?"

She nodded, telling the truth yet omitting her answer to Bryan's invitation. She needed a change of subject. Couldn't risk Luke digging into why Darcy could have refused him if she'd had such a wonderful time.

Maybe it was time to brave another difficult subject. Something she hadn't been able to shake from her mind. "So when are you going to tell me about your conversation with your dad?"

Angling toward her, Luke rested his arm along the back of the glider. He gazed out into the dark backyard, brushing a curl behind her ear as if he didn't realize he'd done it.

He pulled in a deep breath. Looked into her eyes. "He asked me to join his firm."

The air squeezed out of Darcy's lungs. From joy…fear. "Wow."

He laughed, his eyes warm, excited. "I know. That's how I felt."

Had he not told her that earlier, at the hospital, because he thought it might affect her?

Well, of course it would affect her. But would it

really affect her? “Wow,” she said again, unable to think of anything sensible.

“Yeah.” He looked her over, checking out her hair, her dress, even her shoes. “And…” Staring into her eyes, his uncertainty turned to resolve. “And I need to go. You haven’t even had a chance to change yet, fresh off your date.”

Had her date with Bryan influenced Luke’s decision to tell her about the job offer?

No matter, the result was the same. Darcy knew without a doubt she couldn’t simply move on and get over Luke. She could try all she wanted to forget him by going out with other handsome, eligible men. But the truth was, she loved Luke and wanted him.

He stood and offered his hand. She laid her hand in his and allowed him to help her up.

Maybe the lacy dress emboldened her, or maybe it was pure desperation. For whatever reason, she stepped closer to him. “I guess your announcement of the job offer begs the question. What are you going to do?”

“I haven’t decided.” Luke stared into her eyes, and she saw that longing, that heat she’d seen since he’d first arrived.

The connection wouldn’t go away. Yet, he apparently didn’t feel anything beyond the physical attraction, or if he did, he refused to acknowledge it.

"I have to weigh the pros and cons," he said. "Have to evaluate how I feel about…everything."

Was she included in that *everything?* As if she were tossed in there with buildings and business partners?

Apparently so. Iciness gripped her heart. "When will you know?"

"If I were to leave Nashville, I'd have to make a quick decision. Would need to let Roger know something immediately, and then figure out what to do with the building. Moving home would be complicated." He glanced away. "I'd have to be certain."

"I see." *So he's not certain.*

His eyes pled with her, looked apologetic. Was that all Darcy was to him, a complication? Inching away, she tucked away the hurt. Why did she always manage to set herself up for these moments?

"I hope you'll let me know once you decide," she said.

"Of course. I'm glad you understand."

She understood all right. "Thanks for telling me."

Looking relieved, Luke gave her another once-over. "You really do look amazing, Darcy. Gorgeous."

Don't waver. Act normal, so you don't fall apart. Despite the ache his comment caused, she punched him in the arm, old Darcy style. "So much so, that you had to ask who I was when you arrived?"

A crooked smiled formed, lifting one side of his mouth. "I did not ask who you were. I gasped your name, stunned at your beauty."

"I figured I needed to look decent for my big date with Bryan, so Chloe gave me a makeover."

Without looking from her eyes, he took her hand in his, threading his fingers between hers. "You do look amazing and gorgeous all fixed up. Of course, to me, you also looked that way this morning while we were setting up the auction." He lifted her hand to his mouth and kissed her palm. "See you at church tomorrow. I'm glad you had a nice evening."

Luke felt as if his chest might burst. He didn't want to release her hand, but he had to get out of there.

"Yeah, Bryan's a great guy," she said, chin held high.

Sure, she looked beautiful and classy. But he missed the old Darcy. *This* Darcy looked ready to move on to the next phase of her life. And Luke still didn't know what he should do about that.

"Winningham seems to be a decent guy," he said. "You deserve someone who'll treat you well."

"Stop it," she snapped, glaring at him as she planted her hands on her hips. "Just stop it."

"Stop what?"

Anger flashed in her eyes. "I'm sick of hearing you talk about what I deserve. I don't deserve any more than you or anyone else does. I'd just like to think there's someone out there who loves me."

As if embarrassed by her outburst, she mashed a hand over her lips. She appeared hurt.

Lord, I don't feel ready. I don't feel clear direction yet.

As Luke stared into her eyes, he ran a thumb over her smooth cheek.

Oh, there was someone who loved her, all right. And he wasn't out there somewhere.

He was standing right in front of her.

A car door slammed out front.

Luke swallowed words of love—words that would bind her to him, because he wasn't yet sure he was the man she needed. "I think our parents are home from their date."

He had a choice. Tell her how he felt before he was certain he was ready for lifelong commitment, and possibly end up hurting her again. Or watch her jump into a relationship with one of the good guys, one who'd been crazy about her for years.

He hesitated, fear rooting him to the ground.

She stepped away, her expression frosty, distant. "Good night, Luke."

* * *

Darcy slipped inside the house and hurried upstairs, dodging her mom and Burt. With a quiet click, she eased her bedroom door closed and rested her cheek against the cool wood.

The feel of Luke's lips pressed to her palm would be permanently etched in her mind. In her heart.

Her aching, broken heart.

But wasn't this exactly what she'd expected from him?

One more day. If she could make it through one more day, he'd be gone. And then she could fall apart.

Lord, help me get through tomorrow.

Chapter Thirteen

Luke slipped out of the worship service early to do last minute preparation for the auction. He and Darcy were so busy setting out the last of the auction donations and making sure all bid sheets were in place that there wasn't time for any awkwardness.

Until Bryan showed up.

Unable to sleep last night, Luke had lain awake, torturing himself with doubts and questions he hadn't dared ask—didn't have the right to ask. Mainly whether Bryan had kissed her.

With a sick knot in his stomach, Luke watched a small group of fans flock around Bryan. Yet the celebrity drummer's gaze swept the room for Darcy, and he smiled when he found her.

Luke's jaw clenched, and he immediately checked out Darcy's expression.

She smiled and waved when she saw their biggest donor.

Once Bryan extricated himself from the young women following him around, he darted straight over to Darcy.

She looked relaxed, comfortable. Her blush said plenty, too.

Luke had seen all he needed to see and turned away.

He had to be patient. Couldn't jump based on jealously.

Lord, give me wisdom, and certainty.

People began to drift into the fellowship hall, indicating the service had ended. Luke welcomed the Mayor and asked the pastor to say a blessing. Then attendees lined up on both sides of the long tables loaded with fried chicken, salads and every type casserole imaginable. Off to the side, more tables held a variety of desserts, iced tea and lemonade. The whole affair reminded him of all the times his mother had shown up with enough food to feed a small army.

Darcy approached and hooked her arm through his, like she would have done any time in the past. The familiar action felt good, yet he could tell she was preoccupied, had grabbed on to him without thought.

"Once everyone is through eating, do you want to start the welcome and recognition for your mom?" she asked.

"That's the plan."

"Okay." She tried to look perky, but he could tell it was a strain.

"Everything looks great, you two," Noreen said.

"Thanks, Mom." Darcy let go of Luke and followed her mom through the line. Several minutes later, Darcy's small plate of food remained untouched at a table beside Noreen. Never landing long enough to eat, Darcy darted around the room arranging and rearranging items, checking her to-do list, sending him on errands.

Once most of the crowd had finished their meal, Luke went to the microphone to give his grandmother's presentation about the Food4Kids program.

"I'd like to thank everyone for the prayers for my grandmother. She's improving and should be home from the hospital in a few days." The crowd applauded, and he felt their genuine concern deep in his bones. As if this town and church were a part of his makeup, part of his DNA.

For the first time, he truly appreciated this group of people.

Luke read Granny's report on the founding of the organization and the stats of how many kids they'd been privileged to help. Talking about his mother, on top of the recent worry over his grandmother, made him choke up. He had to clear his throat twice to get through the speech.

At a table near the stage, Burt sat with tears in

his eyes. As Noreen took Burt's hand to comfort him, Luke sensed someone at his side.

Darcy didn't touch him, but stood beside him for support. Strengthened by her presence, Luke called the mayor up to make his presentation.

"I'm proud," the mayor said, "to have called Joan Jordan a friend. Proud of her hard work and dedication to the children of our community. Because of Joan, we now have this outstanding program that's serving those most vulnerable." He nodded toward Burt's table.

"Burt, would you please come up and accept this token of our appreciation for your beloved wife and her service?"

As Burt approached the stage to the sound of applause, he beamed with pride.

"Burt," the mayor said, "we've planted a tree outside the courthouse in Joan's memory. The city of Appleton would like to present you with this plaque, a replica of the one that stands beside that tree."

Once again, the audience applauded, and Burt shook the mayor's hand.

Luke glanced at Darcy, smiling.

"This was perfect, Luke," she whispered. "You've truly honored your mom."

"Thank you all for attending and for honoring Joan," Burt said. "As you know, I loved her deeply for many reasons. But mainly because she was a woman of courage and conviction."

Darcy took hold of Luke's hand and held tightly.

Burt gripped both sides of the podium. "When Joan saw a problem, she dove in with a solution. When she saw a need, she filled it. And when faced with a battle, she fought it bravely. I'm thankful that before she fought her last battle with cancer, she fought for the kids in our county. I urge you to bid high today to ensure Joan's work is carried on."

The crowed clapped as his dad returned to his seat.

Contact with Darcy felt good. And right. As if they were meant to work together for the good of a community. *Their* community.

The only time he ever felt at home in his skin was when he was with Darcy. Even as he dated other girls, even as he settled into his new career.

Nothing felt right unless she was involved. Nothing ever would.

The thought slammed into him, stealing his breath away. He loved Darcy O'Malley. *Really* loved her. Not just the emotional, touchy-feely, get jealous of other guys kind of love he'd experienced last night.

But he also loved her with the full commitment kind of love that nothing and no one could change. He loved her with every fiber of his being.

How had he not recognized the fact sooner? Once again, he'd been a fool, had practically pushed her into another man's arms.

Hating to release her hand, Luke gestured to the podium. "Your turn at the mic."

"Thanks." Darcy stared into his eyes then stepped away. She took a moment to thank everyone who donated items for the silent auction, smiling at Bryan as she did so.

Luke squinted his eyes in Bryan's direction.

Game on, drummer boy.

Darcy declared the bidding officially open.

Over the next hour and a half, the proceedings were fun but intense as participants bid on their favorite items.

Despite his jealousy over Bryan, Luke had to be grateful to the musician. The autographed guitar and concert tickets were bringing in big bucks. Several potential buyers kept returning to the bid sheets to raise their bids.

"Amazing, isn't it?" Darcy asked, her eyes bright with excitement.

Luke pointed at the bids. "That guitar itself is going to fund the whole year's budget."

"The man bidding is a collector who heard about the ad and came from Atlanta. He said he knows it'll go up in value once Bryan's band hits it big."

Which was something Luke hadn't really thought much about until he'd seen the crowds of people who'd come for the band's mementos and tickets. Maybe he'd hit on the perfect reason for Darcy to avoid getting serious about Bryan. "Yeah, anyone who marries him would have to move to Nashville and either stay at home while he tours or go on the road with him. Not much of a life for a new bride."

She scrunched her nose, incredulous. "Are you giving me a warning?"

"I'm just telling you what any friend would. I can't see you happy in that kind of life."

In fact, he could only see her being happy with him.

Shaking her head at his declaration, she turned her attention to the bids at the next table and pointed at the two men breathing down each other's necks as the bid on the guitar went higher and higher.

When she smiled, the cute way her nose bunched up pushing her freckles together, reminded him how vulnerable she could be. How tender and sweet.

Loving her would be making a huge step that would change his life.

In an irrevocable but oh, so good way.

"Luke?" Darcy waved her hand in front of his face. "I said I think you need to announce time is nearly up."

Luke shook the wild thoughts from his head and

went to the stage to grab the microphone. "Folks, we're down to the last two minutes. Be sure to check the items you want, to make sure you have the highest bid."

Darcy checked her watch. "Now we get to wrestle the bid sheets away from people when time is up."

Two of the last bidders for the guitar, the local veterinarian who wanted it for his teen daughter and the man from Atlanta, good-naturedly elbowed each other out of the way as they took turns raising their offer.

"Time's up," Darcy called as the wall clock hit bid closing time.

Several groans sounded around the room from apparent losers while others cheered.

"Everyone please go back to the dinner tables while we take up the sheets. Once we have a total, we'll announce the winners, and you can line up to pay and retrieve your items."

The vet had won the guitar. The Atlanta man won the concert tickets. So neither ended up disappointed.

The two women who were Bryan's biggest fans ended up winning the other paraphernalia—autographed drumsticks and concert posters.

The new pediatrician in town, a woman Darcy had called Violet, won the lake house vacation.

Darcy, Noreen and Chloe sat at a table punching in numbers on calculators. Darcy waved Bryan and Luke over.

"Look." Darcy's eyes lit with joy as she showed them the total for the autographed guitar and other items. "Bryan, thank you for helping make this a success."

"I'm glad I could help. I hope you'll invite me back next year."

Darcy and Bryan shared a smile that made Luke's teeth ache.

"You'll be the first I call," Darcy said.

Bryan shook Luke's hand, gave a wave to the O'Malley women and then strode out the door.

"That was a quick departure," Luke said.

Darcy flipped to another bid page, circled the final bid and keyed the amount in her calculator. "He had to get back to Atlanta."

Interesting. And impossible to decipher what his departure meant. Luke was just thankful one distraction was out of the way. It was time for him to make his own bid, to let Darcy know he planned to move back to Appleton to join his dad's firm.

He had to tell her he loved her.

Darcy suddenly hopped up, hurried to the microphone and announced the total money raised for Food4Kids. Cheers broke out through the fellowship hall because they'd well surpassed their goal. She thanked everyone for coming and closed the event with prayer. The day had been a huge success.

Many people had won that day, especially the children in the Appleton community. Plus Joan had been honored, and his dad pleased by the ceremony. Luke had been part of something important, something he'd like to see carried on in the future.

He planned to be right here next year with Darcy by his side.

Before Darcy made it back to the table to begin receiving payments, he snagged her attention. "Darcy, will you go with me to the lake this evening, to get away, relax for a while? You deserve a brief respite."

Her brow furrowed. "I don't think that's a good idea."

Oh, man. Definitely time to pull the friend card one last time. "I need your advice. Really need to talk to my best friend."

She huffed, exasperated.

He couldn't fail. With his best-buddy grin, he bumped her shoulder. "Come on, you know you can't refuse a friend in need."

"We'll see." She hurried away, distracted already by auction duties.

For the first time ever, she hadn't gone immediately into best friend mode. Was she hesitant because of her date last night? Would Darcy give him a chance?

* * *

Darcy walked to her car, worn out but thrilled over the day's results. Luke walked with her, carrying a basket of books she'd bid on and won. Of course, now she needed to make time to read.

He opened her door and set the basket in the backseat. "There you go."

"Thanks. For everything."

His smile, so warm and familiar, set up an ache that was also familiar. Way too familiar.

"I won this basket for Granny." He held up a beautiful handmade basket that held scented bath products. "Please go with me to deliver it. You should be the one to tell her about today."

His acting so polite and sincere meant she simply had to tease him. "Oh, wow, asking nicely and using *please?* I'm stunned."

"Yeah, I've learned when you're tired, you get snippy if I'm bossy."

She laughed as she locked up her car, then followed him to his.

As Luke drove to the hospital, Darcy leaned against the headrest and closed her eyes, taking the opportunity to think.

Should she go to the lake with him? The place was dangerous, full of memories. How could she deal with thoughts of their trip last weekend?

No, she didn't think she could manage to go back to the scene of The Kiss just yet.

Brave the redheaded teen had called her.

No, Darcy wasn't. She wasn't fearless like Chloe.

What *would* Chloe do in this situation? Darcy imagined her with hands jammed on her hips like that day at the café when she shamed the diners, telling Darcy that Luke would leave soon, asking if she was going to just let him go.

Right now though, bravery entailed sitting in the same car with Luke, so close she could smell his shampoo and fabric softener.

Luke wrapped her hand in his, running his thumb against her palm. Her eyes flew open.

"I'm sorry. Were you asleep?"

"No. Just resting." She should pull her hand away. She really should.

Watching his strong profile as he drove, she relished the feel of his warm hand, comfortable in the silence, in his presence, refusing to question his action or her response.

He pulled into the hospital lot and parked, came around to help her out of the car, then reached in the back for Granny's basket. When they got to the room. Grace sat up in bed looking tired but happy to see them. Her color was back to normal, and someone had been by to fix her hair.

Relieved to see her recovering, Darcy's eyes stung. She leaned over and hugged her friend. "I'm so thankful."

"No, dear, I'm the one who's thankful. I hear you may have saved my life."

"I'm telling you, Grace, God was watching out for you. He must have big plans for you yet."

"God was watching out for Granny by sending you," Luke said to Darcy. Then he held the basket aloft. "I won something for you, Granny."

"Oh, I'm going to smell so pretty. Thank you."

He placed it on the windowsill along with several arrangements of flowers.

"Grace, today was amazingly successful," Darcy said. "You'll be pleased to hear we surpassed our budget."

Grace clasped her hands together. "Thank you, God! I'm glad you two came by to tell me."

"We couldn't have done it without your groundwork, Granny. Everyone missed you today."

"I'm thrilled you had a part, son. Your dad called and told me about the memorial for Joan. Thank you for that."

Luke's cheeks streaked with red. "It was my honor. I think it was good for Dad."

"I know it was. Now, why don't you two leave this dreary place and go celebrate."

"I've asked Darcy to go to the lake with me." Luke glanced at Darcy and gave her one of his trademark winks.

"Oh, how nice. Darcy, enjoy yourself. You deserve a nice getaway."

"Exactly," Luke said, his eyes full of mischief. "Darcy, you wouldn't want to disappoint Granny, would you?"

"Are you kidding me?" she asked, yet not really surprised at his ploy. "Playing your sick grandmother to get your way?" she whispered. "Shameful."

"Hey, I'm desperate."

Biting her lip, Darcy tried not to smile at his antics. "I told you, we'll see."

Luke clutched his heart. "You'd leave me in limbo?"

"Go." Grace said. "You two have fun."

As they walked to the car, Darcy decided she would go. But she wouldn't tell him. Would simply leave him to wonder.

The big worry now, though, wasn't about whether to go but, rather, how much she would say when they arrived.

Luke didn't ask again for her decision. He drove to the market and faced her with a big grin. "Need to run and grab a few items for our trip. Be right back." He dashed inside, leaving her in the car with her thoughts.

What truly brave woman ignored her own feelings because she feared the risk of revealing her secret longings? What truly brave woman didn't have the guts to go after what she wanted, *needed.* Wouldn't Darcy tell any other woman in her position that she had a lot to offer and should confidently share her feelings?

Oh, my goodness. I'm that girl. That girl letting mean girls and others tell me I'm not good enough. Worse, I'm telling myself I'm not good enough. Sure, I've been a tomboy and science geek, but I have a lot to offer.

For so much of her life, Darcy had felt invisible, wanting to be valued and loved. When what she'd needed most was to look in the mirror and value herself.

With a confident, somewhat cocky smile on his face, Luke returned to the car and tossed a plastic grocery bag in the backseat. Then he backed out of the parking spot. "Next stop, the lake house."

"Don't you think you're assuming a lot?"

"You want to go to the lake, you know you do."

"You're impossible, Luke Jordan," she said with a laugh.

At a nearby stoplight, he faced her. "Okay, enough joking. I really want you to go. I know you're starving, because at lunch you set down your plate and never ate. So I brought food. I also brought the makings for s'mores since we never got to have them last weekend."

His eyes flashed as he said the latter. Not blame. Something else. Maybe memories? "Darcy, I'd like the chance for a do-over."

Oh, that didn't sound good. A do-over between two friends at an old hangout?

For a moment, her newfound bravery fled. But she could do this. She could prove Chloe and the redhead right.

Besides, Luke had known she hadn't eaten, had worried about her. He was sweet and considerate. "Okay. I'll go."

With a firm nod, and the hint of a smile, he drove out of town, toward the lake. As the buildings of downtown Appleton faded, Darcy stared out the window, watching her reflection when the sun hit just right.

Am I going to let him leave town with a job offer on the table?

Or am I willing to risk my heart once and for all?

Chapter Fourteen

Luke stood hidden at the edge of the woods, peering into the clearing as Darcy gave the logs in the fire pit a poke.

Late afternoon sunlight filtered through the trees, highlighting the lighter, coppery strands of her hair. She still wore the khaki pants and navy polo shirt she'd changed into for the auction.

She was so beautiful, so sweet and generous, that imagining a life with her caused a physical ache in his chest, like pressure from the weight of his future happiness hanging in the balance.

Determination pushed him from the overgrown path, out into the open.

"Fire should be perfect for s'mores soon," Darcy called.

He entered the clearing holding up the grocery bag of supplies. "Still going for the sweets, I see."

"You know me too well."

Never too well. Never enough.

He wanted more than she would ever imagine.

Luke readied the graham crackers and chocolate, then sat beside her on the log, holding a marshmallow over the hot gray coals.

When he got it cooked just the way she liked it, he used his teeth to slip off the burned outside of the marshmallow, leaving the warmly melted inside part. "Exactly the way you like it," he said, handing the treat to Darcy.

Tears pooled in her eyes and quickly overflowed.

"Whoa. What's wrong?" Darcy never cried. Never. "What did I do?"

She hopped up and stood facing him, swiping at the tears as if furious at them for daring to fall.

Luke's lungs squeezed until he couldn't breathe. He stood and ran his hands over her shoulders, smoothing the cottony material. "What's going on?"

She sniffed and dropped her forehead to his chest. "Oh, Luke, I'm making a mess of this."

"Talk to me."

She wrapped her arms around his waist and took several shallow breaths. "You know how I like my marshmallows."

"Yeah."

"No one else knows that. No one. And you don't

even like the burned part." She grabbed hold of his shirt and sobbed, her shoulders heaving.

Wrapping his arms around her, he rubbed her back and kissed the top of her head.

"That's something friends know about each other," he said, knowing good and well he was telling a half-truth. Yes, friends knew that kind of thing.

She was much more than a friend now.

He pulled away far enough to lift her chin and look into her eyes. "Darcy, I—"

"I'm in love with you," she whispered.

Luke stilled. "But—you and Bryan…the date…"

"He did ask me out again. But I told him I couldn't. Because of my feelings for you."

His heart pounded like a gavel to the ribs. He and Darcy had said they loved each other off and on through the years before long trips or extended time apart. As he looked into her eyes, he knew this time she didn't mean the words casually, the way they'd said them their whole lives. The revelation released the vice on his chest, allowing him to take an almost-normal breath.

Sniffing, she swiped at her tears. "Before you made a decision about joining your dad's practice, I had to make sure you knew I love you."

Like warm molasses her words eased inside him, offering healing, peace, contentment. All his life he'd wanted to hear those words from her, and he'd never realized it until this moment. No wonder he'd run anytime he heard the words from anyone else. He'd known the declaration would only mean something coming from Darcy.

Everything finally made sense. The two of them belonged together. Always had.

Tears stinging the back of his eyes, Luke pulled her tightly to his chest.

"I'm sorry," Darcy said, muffled by his shirt, embarrassed to have fallen apart on him.

"Don't be." He swallowed hard, hard enough she could hear it.

Could Darcy do it, take a lesson from Luke's playbook and yank that bandage off, dive right in?

"You know, I used to imagine you were my Prince Charming riding up on a horse—well, bike, and was terrified you'd realize I loved you." Like she was terrified at the moment. Only now, it was a thousand times worse. "I've been crazy about you most of my life."

A slow, tender smile formed and grew until it reached his eyes. He reached out and touched her cheek. "You ruined me for other girls, you know. I ran every time they said they loved me. All because somewhere deep inside, I knew I didn't want those words from them."

She sucked in a breath, and a sense of hope fluttered to life.

He cupped her cheek, running a thumb along her jaw. “I realized earlier today that I’ve always wanted those words from you, only from you. I asked you here so I could tell you.”

Searching his face, she found the smile of her old friend, the same sparkle in his eyes. And also a new contentment and happiness she’d never seen in him before. “What are you saying?” Darcy held her breath, searching his eyes for the truth.

“I love you, too,” he said. “I think I always have. I was just too blind and stupid to know it.”

Her best friend, the love of her life, swooped in, holding her tightly, secure in his arms.

His warm lips moved over hers, kisses interspersed with whispers and promises.

“I was so afraid I would only have that one kiss,” she said, breathless. “Now I want more.”

He rested his forehead against hers. “Me, too. I promise to always be there for you. Please say you trust me to be a better man. Loving you makes me a better man.”

She knew deep inside, at her very core, that he would honor that promise. “Of course I trust you.”

He trailed kisses along her jawline, to her forehead, landing back on her lips. “I want to spend my life here in Appleton,” he said between kisses. “I plan to join my dad’s practice as soon as I’m free to leave Tennessee.”

As her heart soared, she playfully batted her

eyes at him. “So does that mean you’ll be asking me out? On real dates?”

“Definitely. No more of this best friend stuff.” Gazing at her lips, he ran his thumbs over her cheeks and inched his way closer. “We’re a couple now, Darcy. You and me.”

She quickly closed the gap, wanting to shout with the joy and wonder of God’s goodness.

Epilogue

Darcy watched Noreen, who sat at the mirror in the bridal room wearing a cream colored silk suit while Chloe put the finishing touches on their mom's hair. "Mom, you look gorgeous."

"Thank you, honey," Noreen said. "Now, it's time to go. Don't want to keep Burt waiting."

Standing side by side, the three of them looked in the gilt-framed mirror. Chloe and Noreen with their light blond hair and silvery blue eyes. Darcy so different with her dark coppery hair and Dad's deep blue eyes. Three women so different yet each beautiful in her own way.

"Girls, I'm unimaginably happy. And I feel as if your father is looking down on us, giving his blessing."

Darcy nodded, a lump in her throat, tears pooling in her eyes. "I think so, too."

She and Chloe walked arm in arm as they followed Noreen out of the room and to the ceremony. When they arrived at the back of the sanctuary, the wedding director lined them up. Darcy and Chloe would walk their mother down the aisle. Burt and Luke would be waiting.

As the strains of Pachelbel's Canon started and they moved toward the groom, Darcy caught Luke's eye. He was devastatingly handsome in his tux, making her heart flutter with his untamed hair and broad shoulders.

Luke's gaze never wavered as she walked toward him. *I can't believe this man is mine.* As she and Chloe arrived escorting their mother, Luke held out his hand for her. She joined him at the altar as their pastor spoke of joining two families in love and in memory. The three "children" hugged Burt and Noreen and then took their seats.

Granny, as Darcy now called Grace, waited for them in the pew. They joined her and watched together as Burt and Noreen said their vows.

When the service was over, the small gathering of their closest friends moved to the fellowship hall for the reception.

"You look like a princess today," Luke whispered in her ear as they stood off to the side and watched their parents greet guests. His lips wandered to her neck. "And smell good, too."

Would he always make her weak-kneed over

his kisses? "You look so handsome, I'll be fighting off women all day."

He tilted her chin up. "I only have eyes for you." His lips met hers, gently, quickly. "Let's go outside for a minute."

With her heart beating a mile a minute, she followed him to a small garden behind the church. "Now, a proper kiss, please," she said.

"Oh, you know me. I'm all about proper," he said, his voice deep, rumbling.

The man was anything but proper, but she didn't say so as he wrapped her tightly in his strong embrace and descended for a *proper* kiss. A kiss that left her breathless.

"Luke," she said, and it sounded airy.

He growled and raked kisses toward her ear. "Yes, my love?"

"We can't stay out here too long. We'll be missed."

He smiled as he tore his lips from hers. "I'm glad you're keeping me on track." Gazing into her eyes, he took a deep breath and reached into his coat pocket. He pulled out an aged, dried chain of clover.

Her mouth dropped open. "Is that the flower crown I made for you when we were kids?"

"It is. I saved it, pressed in my Bible." He placed it on her head. "I always pictured you wearing it, the princess in those stories you used to tell back when you dreamed of your Prince Charming."

"You said I was crazy. That no guy would ever do something gross like kiss a girl and ask her to marry him."

His smile turned into a wolfish grin. "That was when I thought girls had cooties. Now I find I like the idea of kissing and marriage."

Her very own Prince Charming knelt on one knee. She sucked in her breath, and all her imaginings of knights and princes flashed through her mind.

Luke pulled a small antique-looking velvet box out of his pocket, and she gasped. "What are you doing?"

He flipped open the box, and inside sat his mother's engagement ring, five round diamonds set in a platinum band. A ring Darcy had always admired.

Little did she know all those years ago when he came charging up on his bicycle to protect her, that she'd already fallen for the man she would one day marry.

She blinked away tears, focusing on his earnest expression. "Oh, Luke."

"Darcy, the past couple of months have been the best of my life. But I want more. I want to wake up with you by my side. I want you to have my babies. I want to commit to spend the rest of my life with you, loving you, cherishing you."

Swallowing past the knot in her throat, she nodded. "I want that, too."

"Then will you marry me?"

Darcy's heart filled to bursting. "Yes! Oh, yes." She threw herself into his arms, sitting on his bent knee, and kissed him deeply, once again pouring all her love into it.

He placed the ring on her finger and then caressed her cheeks with warm hands. "I didn't realize what I had in front of me all the time we were growing up. I do now, and I promise to love you as long as I live."

"And treat me like a princess?" she couldn't resist saying, teasing him with his proposal of royal proportions.

He touched the clover crown on her head. "You'll always be my princess."

He was definitely her Prince Charming. Always had been. Always would be.

* * * * *

Dear Reader,

Thank you for taking this journey with me to the fictional town of Appleton, Georgia. I hope you've enjoyed the story of Darcy and Luke, friends who became so much more! As is so often the case, this story was written while God was teaching me about something in my life. At the time the idea took root, God was reminding me that I needed to be fully present in the lives of my family members. You know, sometimes we get so caught up in problems and busyness we forget to appreciate the people right under our noses. God is good and has blessed us with people to love and care for.

I hope reading this story has renewed your desire to be present, to appreciate your family and friends and to reach out in love. Please keep your eye out for my next story set in Appleton!

Thank you so much for reading my book. I love hearing from readers. Please tell me what you think about *The Guy Next Door.* You can visit my website, www.missytippens.com, or email me at missytippens@aol.com. If you don't have internet access, you can write to me c/o Love Inspired Books, 233 Broadway, Suite 1001, New York, NY 10279.

Missy Tippens

Questions for Discussion

1. When the story begins, Darcy O'Malley is struggling to pay off student loans, preparing to support herself. Have you experienced a time when you had your security yanked out from under you or feared change? How did you handle it?

2. Luke Jordan has established a life for himself in Nashville. Do you think he was smart to stay in Tennessee and make his own way? Or do you think he should have swallowed his pride and asked to join his father's practice?

3. What do you think was the theme of this book?

4. Can you think of examples of times you may have taken those around you for granted? If so, what could you have done differently?

5. Why do you think Luke dated woman after woman, always breaking up when one got too serious or mentioned love?

6. Do you think Darcy lacked self-esteem? What do you think parents can do to help build self-esteem?

7. Share about one of your good friends who you can tease with and depend on like Luke and Darcy could with each other.

8. Read and discuss the Bible verse at the beginning of the story. How did it relate to the story?

9. Do you think friendship is a good basis for romantic love?

10. How did you feel about Burt and Noreen's relationship? Did you think their relationship was anyone else's business?

11. Have you ever taken part in a ministry or organization that helped others? If so, describe. If not, can you think of somewhere you can join in to help others?

12. Have you ever met someone like the girl Darcy called the Mean Girl? Why do you think people act like that? How can we have compassion yet stand up for the target of their meanness? Do you think telling someone you love them is risky?

13. Have you ever been striving so hard to succeed

or prove yourself that you lost sight of what's really important? Share what you learned.

14. Who in your life do you appreciate and why? Tell them today!